EAR

Any Other Mouth

Any Other Mouth

Anneliese Mackintosh

**FREIGHT
BOOKS**

First published June 2014
Second edition publised September 2014

Freight Books
49-53 Virginia Street
Glasgow, G1 1TS
www.freightbooks.co.uk

A CIP catalogue reference for this book is available from the British Library.

ISBN 978-1-908754-57-8
eISBN 978-1-908754-58-5

Typeset by Freight in Plantin
Printed and bound by Bell and Bain, Glasgow

the publisher acknowledges investment from
Creative Scotland toward the publication of this book

1. 68% happened.
2. 32% did not happen.
3. I will never tell.

Contents

Anneliese Mackintosh is a graduate of the University of Nottingham and has a Masters degree from the renowned Edwin Morgan Centre for Creative Writing at the University of Glasgow. In 2012 she was shortlisted for the Bridport Short Story Prize and her fiction has been broadcast on BBC Radio 4 and BBC Radio Scotland, published in UK magazines and newspapers *The Scotsman*, *Edinburgh Review*, *Gutter*, and *From Glasgow to Saturn*, and US magazines *Zygote* in my *Coffee*, *Citizens For Decent Literature*, *Big Lucks*, and *Up The Staircase Quarterly*. Anneliese was co-founder of Words Per Minute, the leading Scottish literary club night, and is an Associate Editor of indie publisher Cargo. She lives in Manchester and teaches at the University of Strathclyde.

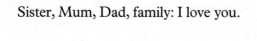

Sister, Mum, Dad, family: I love you.

Messages To My Future Self

When I was eight, I wrote messages to my future self. I stuffed them up the chimney breast, tucked them behind skirting boards, squeezed them between bricks in the cellar wall. I became a genius at finding the places no-one looked.

The idea was this: years later, I'd stumble across the messages, and be reminded of the important things in life. Things like:

If you see litter, pick it up and put it in the bin.

Don't yell at kids for shouting.

Stick up for yourself.

Always keep a notebook handy for ideas, inventions, etc.

Don't have more than one boyfriend at once.

Get a kitten.

*

'Don't work so hard, Gretchen,' said Mum. 'It'll make you ill.'

Actually, I'd been drinking too much, and was getting eczema under my eyes.

Mum suggested I take leave from my admin job and stay with her for a bit. I packed some clothes, a toothbrush, a bottle of whisky and a book on existentialism, and headed for the countryside.

The first day, I got a third of the way through the book on existentialism when Mum asked me to help her make a loaf of bread.

We put 500g of white flour into a bowl, and Mum asked if I was depressed. 'How have you been coping,' she asked, 'since breaking up with Simon?'

I decided not to tell her that I was currently signed up to seven different dating sites, had tried laughing gas in a forest at two in the morning, taken sixty pounds worth of cocaine in one go, slept with two gay women and one gay man, and cried myself to sleep seven nights a week. 'Fine,' I shrugged, putting 40g of butter into the bowl.

'That's a relief,' she replied, adding salt.

I opened a sachet of yeast.

'Pour it on that side,' said Mum. 'Salt kills it.'

I spent the next morning looking at exercise books in the loft. I was amazed to see the stories I'd written as a girl. Gnomes rescuing teddies from factory fires. Charm bracelets growing on trees. Ladybirds playing the flute. Witches with wings.

Where had all the magic gone?

I bashed my head on the roof when I stood up, and grabbed a beam to steady myself. A scrap of paper fluttered to the floor.

Deodorant is bad for the ozone layer. Use soap.

Even if I hadn't just been reading my old stories, I'd have known it was my handwriting straight away. There was a subtle difference between my sister's handwriting and mine. Mine was curvier, maybe. Or the letters weren't as pronounced. It was like the variation between Lottie's bone structure and my own. She had higher cheekbones, a pointier chin, a pixie face. The more camera-friendly version of me. It was the same with our handwriting.

I took the note downstairs and sat on the bed in the spare room, re-reading the words.

I threw away my deodorant.

I went for a jog around the paddocks in my woollen dress. Did twenty star jumps. Tried ten press-ups. Let myself get really sweaty. Finally, I sat beside the apple tree and spoke to my dad's ashes. I told them how I felt – how I *really* felt – about dying.

The smell from my armpits rose to my nostrils.

The following day, while Mum was at her *Colour Me Beautiful* training, I scoured the house. Eventually I found this, tucked behind the Aga:

Don't be with someone you don't love.

When she got home, Mum said, 'I've learnt about summer moving into autumn today.'

I frowned.

'It's a colour thing. People whose skin tones match a summer moving into an autumn palette.'

'Right,' I said, and put the paper in my pocket.

Upstairs, I texted the guy I'd been on three dates with to tell him I didn't love him. I opened the window because my room smelt badly of sweat.

The guy I'd been on three dates with texted back to say he didn't love me either, and asked if I wanted to go bowling next weekend.

I went outside and read some of the book on existentialism aloud to the apple tree. I asked my dad what he made of it, but the apple tree didn't answer.

At dinnertime Mum called me inside and told me she wanted to experiment on me.

'I need to practise before I get real clients,' she said. 'Can I do your colours?'

I sat in a chair for half an hour while Mum held sheets of paper to my face. 'You're a winter,' she announced finally. 'Moving into spring.'

I went to my room and had a cry, then searched behind the skirting board with a safety pin.

Never drink more than two glasses of wine in one day.

I took the bottle of whisky out from under my pillow, and thought about not drinking it. I thought about drinking it. I drank it.

I finished the book on existentialism and listened to the sound of my mother singing a sad song as she washed up, singing Dire Straits to the house, to the walls.

★

These days, I still write messages. Only now I write them to my *former* self, the me I no longer am, the me I'll never be again. But I don't hide them behind the skirting board.

I hide them in the way I walk to the newsagents. The way I flick my head to one side when my picture is taken. The way my eyes widen in the moment before a kiss. I hide them in my laugh. In the food I eat. The words I write. In my bones.

Happiness is beauty.

You are going to hear two different men proclaim that they'd sleep with a pig if it offered. Remember that.

Just because your parents use the mantra NO SECRETS, it doesn't mean there aren't any secrets. And it doesn't make them love you any less.

You are always going to be a winter moving into spring; this is nothing to be ashamed of.

Magic exists. Don't forget where you put it.

What Happens When Someone Dies Twice

My grief is bigger than your grief.

My grief is so big it stretches my skin. My grief is so strong it crushes my bones. So hard it gives me black eyes. So cold I weep icicles. And my grief is so long that it dangles over my food when I'm trying to eat, causing me to throw up onto my plate, and onto my grief.

When it first appeared, I was hanging out the washing. It's amazing what thoughts can creep up on you when you're pegging damp cloth to a line. Mine were: *Fuck. My dad is dead. Forever.* I dropped the pegs, sat on the grass, and wailed.

We didn't have a funeral, because it's Not What He Would Have Wanted. He wanted the hearse to drive him to the crematorium without an audience. He wanted the cheapest coffin and the cross pulled down off the wall, and he wanted to drift down the aisle without anyone watching, to drop into the flames alone.

The problem with this, though, is that the grief had nowhere to go. It welled and it welled, and at the very time his coffin sunk behind the curtain, we were dancing in the kitchen to the Rolling Stones. We laughed, how we laughed, and the grief: it lay low. It bubbled and bubbled, and it kept on bubbling until days had passed, and then weeks.

Eventually, when I was least expecting it, the grief started leaking out. The first place it leaked was in my knickers, and I had to take a spare pair of pants to work. Then the leaking got worse. I never knew grief could make you do that, but I was on the sofa one day, trying to compose an email, and that's when I knew the grief was serious.

I saw counsellors and went to classes. I did therapeutic writing and made a scrapbook. I even stopped pissing and shitting myself, but the grief was still there, leak leak leak, and we would wake up in the morning next to one another – you and I – and you would see the grief, hanging over my head, and it would be very difficult to make love with something so terrible so near us. After a while, we just cuddled instead. Because this is what happens when someone dies twice.

Well, we have been cuddling for seven weeks now, and I think you are starting to get funny about having to share a bed with my grief. I think *you think* it touches me in the middle of the night, that it puts its fingers into the places yours no longer go, makes me shiver and moan and experience the pleasure that I can't reach with you.

But I'm telling you, dearest, this isn't true. I mean, sure, my grief and I have fooled around. I've let it run its glacial palms across my chest, plunge its frosty hands deep inside my pyjama bottoms, and yes, okay, I've let it fuck me and fuck me until I was well and truly fucked and could be fucked no more. But that was just once or twice, and I'm over it now.

Actually, the reason I turn away from you at night, and dig the small of my back into the small of yours—The reason I lie awake, wondering what it might feel like if I gave my grief a razor blade—The reason that I do all this, I realise now, is because my grief is bigger than your grief.

I know you're hiding some on your side of the bed too. I'm certain of that. I saw it sucking you off late one night when you thought I was asleep, and I see it follow you into the shower every morning – small and grey and frail – and I see that it looks a bit like your dead grandma.

But compared to my grief, my love, your grief is shit. It hobbles like a little old lady, a little old lady that lived for eight decades and died peacefully in her sleep. It doesn't make you howl nor gasp nor shriek like mine.

And I just can't help but feel that if I could *beef up* your grief somehow, feed it and make it grow until it was at least five times the size – then maybe you and I could finally make love once more.

With that in mind, I've been thinking about poisoning your parents.

We could invite them over for dinner next week, and I would serve them The Special Two Slices of Pie. It would be sometime during Trivial Pursuit that they'd grab one another. They'd convulse and bleed, leaving their Science and Nature question completely unanswered, and the game would, inexorably, be over.

I've thought about your sister too. She's pregnant right now, with a foetus of just six fragile months. Her death would be doubly tragic. And I've thought about your aunt, your uncle, your godfather, your piano teacher, your best friend.

Wow.

If I play my cards right, your grief has the potential to grow enormous. Given time, it might even be able to teach *my* grief a thing or two.

We could go on holiday, me and you and our respective griefs, and we could drink Sangria and hang out at the beach, maybe even learn a New Thing together, like surfing or chess or the Kama Sutra.

Then, in the evenings, after a long day of fucking, we could sit on our balcony under the light of the moon and cry. And as we cried, we could look through the salt of our tears, across the sea and into the blackness, and we wouldn't need words any more, because the shadows at our sides would be enough, and we would be enough, and the whole world, as it was, would be enough.

Crave

You're dead to me.

That's how it starts. Sarah Kane's words, not mine.

And actually, that's not how this story started. More how it ended. What happened, to begin with, was this.

Nottingham University. The most popular school of English in the country. In the top ten on *The Times* league table. A ratio of two girls to every boy.

Frances was a dancer. She was slim and tall, with pale skin and auburn hair. She wore tight clothes, clothes which I could never wear, and her body moved with a grace I would never know.

I was in a play, and Frances was producing it. Why she was producing a play and not onstage herself was a mystery. I saw her dance plenty of times, and it was amazing. When she was waiting for the bus, she danced. When she was queuing for a cup of tea, she danced. When she was lying in bed, she danced. Yet for some reason I couldn't quite fathom, she never joined a class or tried out for a musical. Frances was a secret dancer, and only I, and those who queued with us at the bus stop or in the canteen, knew it.

We were members of the theatre society. By day, we were all engineers or philosophers or biochemists, but by night, we took over the empty seminar rooms around campus, and we came alive. We became Macbeths and Goldbergs, Nells and Miss Prisms. We climbed out of rubbish bins and into dolls' houses. We developed limps and lisps, and drank endless decanters of apple juice. We became our hopes, our dreams, our nightmares. We became anything other than ourselves.

I'd never done any acting before I came to university. I'd arrived on campus brimming with Kafka, Eugenides and Hesse, but found myself in a world of Austen, Caedmon and Pope. So when a friend from halls asked if I minded missing my nine o'clock *Beowulf* lecture to accompany her to the theatre tryouts, I obliged. Full of the joys of skiving an hour of Anglo-Saxon tragedy, I even tried out myself.

And that's how I landed Ophelia in *Hamlet*. Complete fluke. I don't know what it was. They must've sensed something in me. Some sort of fucked-up-ness that told them I couldn't just *play* Ophelia, I was Ophelia.

Yes, I was someone who knew what it was like to talk in riddle and rhyme, to disgrace myself at a party, to be spurned by a lover and go mad with grief. And because it was a modern-day version of *Hamlet*, I even got to wear my own clothes, to show my piercings and expose my tattoo. It was the best and scariest and most exciting thing I'd ever done.

Lottie had to sit in the car for the second half because of the self-harm. I'd forgotten to mention it to my parents until we went out for lunch earlier that day. 'It'd be best she doesn't see it,' they said, and my sister cried.

But the main thing was, I was an actress, darling. I had someone fall at my feet after my final performance. I went out to nightclubs and gave guys handjobs in the loos because they recognised me. And, just as I finished, some other man would come up to me with this look in his eye, and he'd say, 'It's you. You're Ophelia.' And I would curtsey and smile, and then give him a handjob too, if he wanted. I was a celebrity. I could do anything. Anything you wanted.

By the second year of university, I'd really got a name for myself: Disturbed Girl. That's how I got to play C in *Crave*. She was even more unhinged than Ophelia. I'd stood in the audition and I'd let my soul come out. I'd gnashed my teeth, grabbed my hair, and if it wasn't so *terrible* then you might have been mistaken in thinking I was having an orgasm. But I wasn't to know what one of those felt like for several years yet, so in the meantime, I was just showing those gaudy theatre types how fucking fucked-up I could be. Exactly what it meant to grow up in the middle of nowhere, with unhappy parents, and a sister with psychosis, and that thing that happened, that atrocious thing that I couldn't quite remember, but it had left me with a big black hole in the middle of my stomach, leaving me empty inside: a skin, a husk, nothing.

So yeah, I got the part.

The play was by Sarah Kane. I'd never heard of her before, but I knew from the audition that she was like me. I only saw a few lines of the play (a lot of which were recycled from other sources, including *The Waste Land* by T. S. Eliot, which I should have been familiar with, but had slept in for the lecture), yet even going by the small amount I did see, I knew. Kane hated. She loved. She felt. But, most importantly, she hated.

When I found out I'd been cast, I went out to celebrate. Drank five pints of snakebite. Snogged my goth friend Fi, groped my goth friend Phil, and everyone was so pleased for me. I requested my favourite song by Sepultura, which the DJ didn't play, and I moved off the snakebite and onto the 3-for-2 Reefs at the Student Union. I strawpedoed them. I threw up.

The first rehearsal was terrifying. Four actors, and all four of us, we were informed, were to stay onstage for the full forty-five minutes. Lines were to be battered out in quickfire. There was no setting and no plot.

We sat cross-legged in the middle of a Philosophy seminar room in the Portland Building, and introduced ourselves: A, B, M, and C. Our voices shook as we read.

The director, a second-year Sociology student called Michael, wore trousers that were slightly too short for him, and had a beard that was slightly too long. He adjusted his crotch whenever we read the lines about rape, and I occasionally worried about his mental health.

In the second week of rehearsals, he introduced us to Frances.

'Frances will be producing the play for us. She's in charge of costumes, make-up, booking rooms, things like that.'

'Hi,' said Frances, curling her hair around her forefinger. She told us she was a Criminology student, and that she liked hip-hop and ballet. She had goosebumps and an honest smile.

With Frances there, we had someone new to impress, an audience. We stood there in that rehearsal space, which, by day, was Geography seminar room E42, yet, that night, seemed like The Globe or The Old Vic. I could sense a change in all of us. A was moodier; the most aggressive rapist he had ever been. B was colder, his words cutting into us like shards of ice. And M: well, M was more maternal. Like she was about to rip off her V-neck top and force our hungry mouths onto her nipples there and then.

Afterwards we went out to a pub in Hockley. Tall leather seats, jazz, cheap drinks. We talked about Sarah Kane. 'She's dead,' said A. 'She was crazy,' said B. 'A lesbian,' said M.

The director, Michael, stayed quiet. He sipped his Bacardi and coke and watched us, his actors, and somehow I sensed that he was touching himself under the table.

While the others were all at the bar, Frances edged around the seats towards me. 'Let's fuck!' she shouted. At least, I think that was what she shouted. There was a saxophone an inch from my ear.

'What?' I called back.

'I want to be fucked!' she shouted.

We looked at each other – a difficult look – as if our eyes had to fight their way past all that sound. I took her hand. It was my turn to get goosebumps.

We got a taxi back to mine. I showed her my bedroom, and she told me we had the same pillowcases. We lay on the sheets and looked at the moon through the skylight and she confessed to me that she was a virgin.

It wasn't the fact she was twenty-one that surprised me about this, but the fact that she seemed so confident in her own body. The way her limbs moved, the way she conducted herself, I assumed she must be a pro between the sheets. She was a dancer, for god's sake. I was a geeky English Literature student.

We took off our dresses and laughed. 'Are you a

lesbian?' I asked.

'No,' she replied. 'I'm straight.'

I propped myself up on one elbow and looked her in the eye.

'I'd love to have sex with you,' she sighed.

So I reached around her back and took off her bra, and began to make tentative love to her, running my fingers over her soft skin, touching her ever so gently, and then grabbing her, great handfuls of her, until I was plunging myself into her so hard she screamed.

The rehearsal the next day was weird.

Without alcohol, our barriers were back. Frances excused herself to go next door and make phone calls. She was trying to locate matching black t-shirts for us all, she said, and it was proving difficult. I noticed some negative energy flowing between A and M, and wondered if they'd been at it last night too. Poor B looked a bit miffed – I knew he'd had a thing for M since they were in that last play together, *Habeus Corpus*, and he was playing Dr. Wicksteed in pursuit of the young, nubile Felicity Rumpers. But he'd never got her in that play, and alas, I knew, he'd never get her in this.

'Right, gang,' said Michael. That's what he called us: gang. 'We're going to start off with some trust exercises today.'

'Catching each other?' asked A.

'No bloody way,' said M, casting him a dark look.

'I'm up for it,' chirped B.

We spent the next fifteen minutes falling, catching, falling catching. I didn't mind the falling. Falling I had no problem with. Ask me to fall, and I'd fall every time. I'd fall if there was no-one to catch me.

Catching, on the other hand, was hell. What if I couldn't do it? What if I felt the weight of another human being pushing into me and I just... crumpled? I hated trust exercises because I didn't trust myself.

After that we did a full run-through. No actions today, just standing still and getting the lines right.

No.

Yes.

No.

Yes.

No.

No.

Yes.

The intonations, the repetitions, the rhythm. The bit where each of us emits a [*short one syllable scream*]. The bit where I emit a [*formless cry of despair*].

'What exactly does a formless cry of despair sound like?' I asked Michael.

'It's just... formless,' he replied.

I hadn't tried this part of the script yet. We'd read it out as a stage direction whenever we reached it in previous run-throughs.

'Make a noise,' said Michael. 'Go for it. I'll tell you afterwards if it's right.'

So I took a deep breath, opened my mouth and let the sound come out, snaking out from the pit of my lungs, slow, coiling, until it became a howl, a low throb, and finally a moo. That's right, I was a cow when I did my formless cry of despair. A cow standing in an abattoir, the second before its throat gets slit.

'Was it alright?' I asked.

They all looked, and nodded.

After the rehearsal, Frances came up to me. I stared at my phone, pretending to be busy sending a text, though really I was just pressing the number three.

'I think I'm falling in love with you,' she said.

I pressed three a few more times. 'You're what?'

'I'm falling in love.'

Nobody had ever said this to me before. My cheeks flushed. 'Want to go back to mine?' I asked.

That night we took things slow. I showed her exactly where I liked to be touched. How long I like to be touched in each place. How many times I like to be circled with a tongue. Where I like to feel the pulse of a forefinger, and at what point I wanted her to thrust inside me, to pin me down and make me shout.

Afterwards, I did the same thing to her, talking her through it all over again, teaching her to have sex with me, teaching her to have sex like me.

And for that reason, although we tried all night long, and the sheets were soaked in sweat, neither of us managed to come.

If I could be free of you without having to lose you.

I spoke my lines in bed, the shower, under my breath, out loud. I needed to get them perfect. It wasn't Michael who was putting the pressure on us. 'We all make mistakes,' he would say. 'Cancel and continue. Cancel and continue.' But I didn't want to make mistakes. I didn't want to cancel.

I wanted to continue, continue, continue.

You get mixed messages because I have mixed feelings.

I stopped eating because I felt that C wouldn't eat. C would starve. C would crave. C would emit formless cries of despair. I felt more like myself than I had ever done. The most I ate in a day was a tin of sweetcorn.

Don't die.

I need a miracle to save me.

Outside, a man was yelling. There were no words, not that I could make out, just sounds. Was he in pain? Angry? I was lying in bed and couldn't be bothered to get up and look out of the window to find out.

Frances was still sleeping, her chest rising and falling with heavy breaths. As I ran my fingers down her arm, over the thin red hairs, I realised that I was growing scared of her.

I don't know if it's because she reminded me too much of what I was not: elegant, innocent. Maybe it was because I feared that she would soon overtake me. Everything I had taught her, she had been learning just like her dance moves. She wanted to practise each new motion over and over: circle, pulse, repeat, circle, pulse, repeat, until she had memories in her fingers. Now, when she touched me, she didn't have to think any more. She let her instincts take over, let the choreography take care of itself, while she whispered the strangest, most erotic, most frightening things in my ear.

Actually, what scared me about her most, I think, was this: Frances had become the best person at having sex like me there was. Better than me at being me.

I look at the large beige hessian cushion, try to connect, try to decipher myself woven into the clean blank fabric.

I kept searching for excuses not to see her, and failing.

And then at the paisley green cushion, a thoroughly inappropriate cushion to represent any part of me, especially the parts I am showing to her.

'I love you,' she told me. 'I'm in love with you.'

You've fallen in love with someone that doesn't exist, I murmured. No, that's not right.

I stopped going out. After rehearsals, the rest of the cast would head out for a film, or a beer, or ice skating, or jazz, and I would shake my head, say I needed some rest, and slink back home in silence. Frances would come to me at two or three in the morning, smelling of booze, stroking my hair and giving me kisses.

Not this time.

The formless cries were taking it out of me. They rose up from such a deep place inside me now, that even just one a night was too much. Often we had to repeat the play four, five times in a row. Five cries of despair. I thought I might be dying.

Not yet.

At the end of each run-through, my t-shirt was soaked with tears and snot.

I am an emotional plagiarist.

'M fancies A,' B said to me one evening, during the break.

'Of course,' I replied. 'It's obvious.'

'Oh,' he sighed, then looked at me in a way he'd never done before. 'And you...? Are you–'

'No,' I told him. 'I'm taken.'

By the week of the performance, we were slick. We stood in a circle, holding hands, saying the words over and over. B, M, C, A, B, A, B, C. No time for pauses: as soon as one line finished the next person picked it up. It was throw and catch, throw and catch, throw and catch, not one single fall. And yet I was falling. Falling and falling.

[*Emits a short one syllable scream.*]

I took Frances by the hand each night, kissed her fingertips, let my tears fall onto her breasts, forced her inside me, four fingers at a time. I told her I loved her, told her I hated myself, that I couldn't be with her, that I needed her.

[*Formless cry of despair.*]

She whispered into my ear that I was perfect. Brilliant. Top-notch. The best. But that she and Michael were in a relationship now. That she'd taught him just how to touch her, how many times to circle, pulse, repeat. She plunged her fingers into me, in and out, in and out, still never quite making me come, and told me that the time was right for her to spread her wings. That she'd never forget me. Thank you for everything. One last pirouette, and then– *You're dead to me.*

I cried onstage in front of fifty strangers. I gnashed my teeth and pulled my hair. *I feel nothing, nothing. I feel nothing.*

And there was Frances on the front row, holding Michael's hand, pulsing, pulsing, pulsing into his palm.

In den Bergen, da fühlst du dich frei.

I could see Michael, touching himself as we said our lines, the tautness of his trousers, there at the crotch.

Free-falling.

Into the light.

Building up to our final crescendo.

Finishing not at all where we started.

Happy.

Desperate.

Happy and free.

Daddy Smokes

'Wannabe' by the Spice Girls is playing on tape cassette.

I had to beg Dad to switch off 'Gardeners' Question Time' and put this on instead, so I'm surprised that it's playing for something like the tenth time in a row and nobody's sick of it yet. In fact, it's quite the opposite. Posh, Ginger, Baby, Sporty, and Scary – without knowing it – are bringing me, my dad, and my sister closer together. Something in their song is making us feel, with each new chorus, that we're more connected than ever before.

To help us savour this moment, my sister and I decide to write down the lyrics. Lottie reaches into the boot of the car and gropes for Dad's holdall in search of a pen. Moments later, she recoils.

'There are cigars in his bag,' she whispers.

I look at Dad, driving us around the streets of Skegness, with his greying hair and snuggly jumper, and I want to tell Lottie that she must be mistaken. Of course there aren't cigars in his bag. Daddy doesn't smoke. No secrets in our family, remember? No secrets.

But I don't tell Lottie a thing. I just ask Dad to switch up the music.

I'm fourteen now. While my peers are chasing boys, learning to apply lipstick, and maybe even having sex, I'm at home, sitting on the upstairs landing with a notebook. I've drawn three columns.

Out | In | Details

In the first column, I write down the time that Dad goes out of the back door. I watch him cross the lawn and disappear out of view.

In the second column, I note the time he comes back.

The final column is for recording unusual behaviour. Fiddling with something in his jacket pocket. Looking nervously from side to side. His coat smelling of smoke when he comes back in. You have to be careful with that one, though, because Dad often smells of smoke. Every few days, he lights bonfires behind the caravan at the end of the garden. He'll watch the rubbish burn for hours.

Currently, I'm waiting to fill in the final two columns. Dad's been in the garden for over half an hour. As I doodle stars and spirals on the corner of the page, I decide that, with a notebook full of evidence in front of me, I'm going to have to face facts.

So I've had sex by now.

Quite a lot of sex, with quite a lot of boys. The one I'm with at the moment, Sam, has just poured exploding candy onto his tongue and licked me while I popped.

We've come outside to have sex again. Neither of us have ever done it *al fresco*, and, since we seem to be the only ones in the world who haven't, we wander around the garden looking for a good spot: one where Mum won't catch us.

I suddenly think of the caravan.

Strictly speaking, I'm not supposed to go in there. It was here when we bought the house and it's old and falling apart – Dad says it's dangerous.

A rusty pipe wedges the caravan door shut. I yank it out of the ground and we're greeted by damp and dust. The floor caves under my weight; even more so when Sam joins me. We stand still for a moment, listening to each other's heartbeats. Then Sam grins and beckons me into the back. I stay where I am, transfixed by the kitchenette: the yellow Formica, peeling back to reveal rotting wood and wormholes, and the sink... the sink is full of grey powder. I can smell it. Cigar ash.

'Fuckin' hell, Gret!' shouts Sam. 'Come and look at this.'

Swallowing away a burning in my throat, I go into the back. Sam is waving something in the air.

'Porno!' he shouts.

He's holding a magazine displaying a brunette with massive breasts and a leather whip, and he points to an open cupboard door. I manoeuvre around broken glass and decaying wood to look inside.

There must be getting on for a hundred magazines in there. I lift spines to reveal covers, and words jump out at me. *Lesbians. Teachers. Secretaries. 50s and Over. Schoolgirls.* Every issue is dated within the last year.

'Fuck!' Sam laughs behind me, and pulls a fold-up mattress out from the caravan wall. It's worn, but much cleaner than everything else in here. 'A fuckin' bed!'

I perch on the edge of the mattress. Instead of having sex, Sam and I begin to work our way through the magazines. I have never seen pornography before, and it feels worlds apart from the white knickers and popping candy Sam and I have just experienced. I didn't realise that so many girls shaved themselves down there for a start. And what about their labia: where are they? Is my vagina, you know, alright?

I don't know what it is exactly, but as I'm screwing up my eyes at the glossy pages, I'm feeling something I've never felt before. A mixture of disgust and excitement.

I throw the magazines in the cupboard and tell Sam to go home.

Later that night, I can't stop thinking about those women, peeling themselves open with their fingers. They're nothing like the Scary and Sporty Spices I used to compare myself to as a young teen. I sit on the carpet, legs apart, peering into a handheld mirror. But neither the Spice Girls nor the porn stars look anywhere near as Scary as I do when I see myself properly for the first time.

Mum is making lasagne, and I've finally built up the courage to speak to her.

'I don't mean to worry you,' I start, 'but did you know that Dad keeps a load of porn in the caravan?'

She puts down her knife and turns to me.

'Porn?' she blurts. 'Oh, I've been in porn!'

She tells me that she once had a Polaroid printed in the *Playboy* 'Readers' Wives' section, as a present for Dad. She laughs, almost uncontrollably, then goes silent. After warning me not to mention it to my sister, she turns back to the sideboard, and her head hangs as she chops onions.

I'm eighteen and I can do anything. Currently I'm doing anything in New Zealand, travelling the world on my own. It's been my first day aboard the Kiwi Experience bus, and we've stopped at a hostel for the night. The bus-driver-cum-holiday-rep, Dangerous Dave, has put us into pairs – boys with girls – and we've been given an instruction. The boys have to wear the girls' clothes, and the girls have to wear bin bags.

The other girls at the hostel fashion their bags into tight black dresses or skimpy bikinis. I've simply stuck three holes in mine – one for my head, two for my arms – and I'm wearing it like a sack of shit. Feels good to be different.

By the time it hits midnight, I'm trashed. I cross the room and put a coin in a slot. I lick my lips and pull a lever.

Then I walk over to the guy who's wearing my miniskirt and my make-up. I push him onto a chair, straddle him, and light a cigar.

Dad is dead and we're at a fancy restaurant.

I live in Scotland now, and it's the first time Mum has come to visit me in two years. She stayed at home a lot in the late stages of Dad's illness. She'd sit on the sofa, watching TV, while he sat on a sun-lounger on the patio, smoking cigars.

The last time I saw Mum, we were scattering Dad's ashes in the garden. They were still hot from the furnace, and we tipped them out of his old Wellington boots onto all his favourite places. The last place we sprinkled them was the bonfire.

Today, I take Mum to a restaurant in the Merchant City. I order smoked mackerel pâté to start, and she has a salad. When I get to my final mouthful, she says, 'That'll repeat on you all day now.'

Then she begins to talk.

She tells me about the holiday I had in Skegness when I was thirteen. That she told Dad to take me and my sister on that trip. That she'd found Dad in bed with the local barmaid, and needed some breathing space. That she'd always had to compete with other women for Dad's attention. That he'd never made her feel like she was *enough*.

I'm trying to take in what she's saying, but I can't escape the taste of mackerel and the sound of 'Wannabe' playing in my head like a backing track.

Mum's getting the caravan demolished. She's selling the house and wants it gone. Some travellers say they'll do it for two hundred quid. She'll pay them at the end, she says, as long as they do a good job.

Once done, the travellers call her into the garden. As Mum examines their work, they tell her that, as the caravan came crashing down, a load of pornographic magazines came tumbling out.

'Some of them are quite recent,' they remark.

She hands over the money and bites her lip, trying to fight the urge to ask them *how recent*.

That evening, Mum is in the garden with her new boyfriend, David. He's helping her do the place up, to increase the market value. They've taken more than twenty wheelbarrow-loads of rubbish to the bonfire today, and they're exhausted.

Sometimes the rubbish from the bonfire topples down,

and they push their spades into the ground to shovel it up and add it to the heap once more. Now and then, where David's spade hits the ground, he comes across a jagged, half-buried bin bag. He heaves it out of the earth, and discovers a pile of magazines inside. Peeping out between grimy pages: a catalogue of naked breasts and hairless vaginas.

David doesn't say anything whenever this happens, but he keeps on digging, putting each new unearthed bag on top of the bonfire in silence. Mum stands behind him, equally silent.

Later, they light the bonfire. The bin bags melt in the heat. Flames devour the schoolgirls and the secretaries, alongside the worm-eaten wood from the caravan, weeds from the front garden, juice cartons from the kitchen, and the old, beat-up sun-lounger from the patio. The whole lot goes up in smoke.

There are so many fumes, in fact, that the nearest neighbour in the hamlet – who lives half a kilometre away – complains that the smoke is going into her house.

'It's going into *my* house too,' Mum says, 'but I can't help it.'

Before the house is sold, I go back to stay one last time.

I take a walk around the garden, and, under the elderflower bush, I spot a charred, damp scrap of paper. There's a naked woman and a phone number on it. The woman's face has been partially burnt off. I kneel on the soil while I look at her, and, after several minutes, I have my first orgasm. It's shaky and lonely and filled with grief.

Then I wander down to the pond, thick with algae, to

the chicken coops, overgrown with weeds, and finally to the bonfire. It's funny really – when I look at it, I can no longer tell which parts of the grey dust are porn, which are cigars, and which are my dad. But even though the smoking has stopped, I know that all of them, once, glowed red.

Somebody Else's Story

We met in 1967. At the start of that year, The Monkees got to number one with 'I'm a Believer', and by the end, it was The Beatles with 'Hello Goodbye'. But it was just before that, in November – when Long John Baldry was at the top of the charts with 'Let the Heartaches Begin'– that I met your mother.

It was at a school dance. I went to the boys' grammar on one side of the road, and your mum went to the girls' school on the other. Once a year, every year, the boys and girls came together for three hours of whispering, giggling, and ironically 'doing The Freddie'.

That year, the dance was being held at the girls' school. I'd been given the task of hanging the decorations that the girls had spent the last fortnight making. I was halfway through putting up the streamers when I saw her.

'Hello, bluebird,' he said to me.

He was standing on a ladder with his arms in the air. I remember his corduroy shirt and giant grin. He looked older than me – I couldn't tell how much – but I thought he was very handsome.

I wished I'd had time to take off my glasses. I always took them off after school, in case boys saw me. Caught the wrong bus home several times; ended up getting off the other side of Stretford. It was silly of me to be so vain, really, but when you've got spectacles on your face, a brace on your teeth, and corrective shoes on your feet, you're not exactly going to have boys running down the street after you.

But here he was. A real life boy, looking straight at me, so I smiled back at him. I even let my braces show.

She was so petite, your mum, with a pretty, dainty little mouth and a rebellious splash of freckles around her eyes. I wanted to twirl her round and kiss her.

We danced that night, to the Bee Gees, The Monkees, and the Rolling Stones.

And I ended up kissing that lovely little mouth.

When he first told me, I couldn't believe it. I looked into the living room mirror, saying it: 'He loves me, he loves me!' I did cartwheels on the front lawn.

I kept her a secret from my parents for as long as possible.

'She's common,' they said after meeting her. 'She doesn't speak properly and she eats chip butties.'

'I know,' I smirked.

His family were descended from aristocracy. Mine couldn't

afford stockings so they used to paint their legs with gravy.

He told me he was related to Lord Byron. I didn't know who that was. I was descended from Maltese pirates. My great-great-grandmother murdered her husband for adultery.

Every time she came to mine, my parents would follow us around the house. They'd sit outside my bedroom door, tutting. I don't think they ever offered her so much as a cup of tea. So normally we went to her parents' house. We had cups of tea and privacy there.

I remember one evening, during our first summer together. We'd just had corned beef hash, then we went for a stroll along the golf course. I could still feel the sugar on my teeth as we walked. Now and then your dad would let go of my hand and run ahead. 'Come on, slow coach!' he'd laugh. He'd run back and tickle me until I screamed.

At the golf course, we sat by a tree and watched some old men playing at hole thirteen. We listened to the quietness for a while, and I realised how happy I was to be here – happier than I'd been with any of the other girls. I wanted to do everything for your mum, you know. I really did.

What I didn't want was to go home and face my parents. Would they smell corned beef on me? I didn't want to go home to my English homework either. Loved reading, but hated analysing the stuff afterwards. It just didn't make sense. All opinions, no right or wrong. Maths and Science: they were the things that excited me. What excited me was perfect sense.

'See that bush?' your mum asked suddenly, pointing to a prickly hedge with wild blackberries growing between the leaves. I nodded. 'I used to have a den in there. There were three of us in the gang. We used to hide in there and tell each other secrets.'

'Well?' he shouted, jumping up again. 'What are we waiting for? Let's go!' He ran over to the hedge, pulled back the brambles, and stuck his head between branches.

I ran after him, grabbing at his t-shirt. 'You'll get scratched!'

Somehow we managed to climb inside. I was surprised she followed me in there, to be honest. I tended to do these things on impulse – having fun just made perfect sense. But my idea of entertainment wasn't necessarily anyone else's.

I was breathing so fast I could hear my heart beat. I certainly did some strange things for this boy. I guess, even though I was only fourteen, I was madly in love. Sometimes that's the only explanation you need.

'So,' I said, taking her hand. 'I know we're one person short – there are meant to be three of us – but is this okay?'

'Course,' she replied, brushing a twig off my lip.

'Jolly good,' he said, sounding like something straight out of one of his Famous Five books. 'So now we need to tell each other our secrets.'

Her eyes widened. She had such rebellious freckles around her eyes. Did I tell you that already? I fell in love with her because of those freckles.

'You go first,' she whispered.

He took a deep breath and made a low hum. 'Alright,' he said eventually, 'here's my secret.'

He shifted a little closer, and let his knees touch mine.

'I think,' he said quietly, 'my mum's an alcoholic.'

I bowed my head, let the information sink in. He'd told me a real secret. My friends – back when it was me and Jenny and Maeve in the gang – we didn't tell secrets like that. We told secrets about which boy you fancied. Whose homework you'd copied. Which girl in your class you hated most. But that was three years ago; this was now.

'Go on,' he urged, perhaps regretting having given so much away. 'It's your turn.'

'Okay,' I replied. I put my lips to his ear.

I got used to being in confined spaces for a while after that. Crouched in the attic, with a torch and a couple of Beano annuals. Pissed in an old milk bottle.

A few months later, I was back at school. I'd missed so much work. I felt really stupid. All those weeks of hiding away in my bedroom, and lying on my back looking up at the hospital ceiling. It didn't give you a thirst for knowledge. I was doomed to fail my Maths O-Level, as you know, five times before I passed.

But I don't think I was as stupid as you've always thought. I was hurt, but I wasn't stupid.

I came down from the attic after three days. Mum and Dad were going crazy. Mum was drinking more than ever. She warned me to stay away from your mother for good.

Which, of course, made me determined to see her.

It took a long time for things to get back to normal. But by the following summer, we were walking on the golf course again, laughing and chasing each other. He was saying he loved me, and I was saying I loved him.

Everything felt good. 'Young Girl' had been at the top of the charts for four weeks straight, but was about to get knocked off the number one spot by The Rolling Stones' 'Jumpin' Jack Flash'. I would be finishing school in just one more year, and I'd even got myself a scooter with the money I'd been saving up from my paper round. Always a good idea to have transport. So much more freedom.

I mean, he still messed up sometimes. He'd do something bad, something ridiculous, like this one time, when we went out for some food, our first time in a restaurant together, and he didn't have enough money to pay the bill. He climbed out of the toilet window and left me to deal with the consequences.

Or I'd see him after school, his arms wrapped around

someone else. Then he'd spot me and run over. Hold me tight and tell me I was the only one.

Like I say, I wasn't stupid.

When I got upset, he'd be so apologetic. He'd sit in the street on his scooter, singing songs outside my bedroom window. Sometimes he even brought a guitar. I always forgave him when he did that. Even though it usually ended with my dad going downstairs, shouting: 'Get out of it, you big drongo!'

Eventually, I plucked up the courage to propose. I'd been an idiot for long enough, and I knew she loved me. It just made perfect sense.

'We should get married,' I said, as I walked through the door. I'd never seen her happier.

The preparations were going great, until he went missing.

Eleven weeks before they found him. He was making a living as a factory worker in Bradford. Said he was seeing a psychiatrist.

I pawned my engagement ring and started saving up for a ticket to America. I'd heard you got treated well over there, that it was a good life, being a nanny. Funny to think now, that it never happened, but that you were brought up by so many different nannies when you were a little girl.

I'd rather not talk about Bradford.

I was lying in bed one night, wondering what else to pawn so I could afford that ticket. Just as I decided to sell my sewing machine, my one last possession of worth, I heard a scooter drive into our street.

Best decision of my life.

I drew back the curtains and there he was.

Strumming a guitar.

Jumpin' Jack Flash.

I meant it, you know.

He meant it.

We got married three weeks later.

His parents said they'd give us a year.

We lasted thirty-four more.

When I Die, This Is How I Want It To Be

When I die, I don't want a religious ceremony. I want a humanist service, preferably; just a simple room where a few folk gather together – and cry a little – as my coffin is brought in. I'm not fussy.

The coffin needn't be extravagant. The cheapest one they do at The Co-op is fine. That's what I got for my dad's funeral last year – corrugated cardboard, with a plastic lining – and that was expensive enough. As for coffin-bearers, well, normally there are six, so I suppose my six most recent lovers will do. They'll probably be quite happy to feel the weight of my dead body in their hands.

Even though I want you to burn me, I still want dressing up first. I'd like to go smart-casual. You know, dressed-down enough to acknowledge the occasion. I mean, nobody's under any false pretences here: I'm dead, and I'm about to be incinerated. I don't need shoes. And you can dispense with mascara, since my eyes will be shut. But I'd still like to make a bit of an effort. A nice dress, new pair of tights. Touch of lipgloss. And that silver ring my sister made me in psychiatric hospital, on a chain around my neck.

I'd like to be holding a book. *Revolting Rhymes*, ideally, but I'm flexible as long as it's in Roald Dahl's canon. I'd like a David Bowie CD with me too, and a picture of my family before we fell apart. Oh and a Swiss army knife, in case I need it in the afterlife. I'm a staunch atheist, so I'm fully expecting to go to hell.

Just before I disappear behind the curtain and – poof – I turn to dust, I'd like Stephen Hawking to give a small speech about the beginning of the universe. I'd like him to demonstrate, in a few short paragraphs, just how insignificant my life has been, in the great scheme of things.

Then I'd like the-woman-who-offered-me-a-bite-of-her-Mars-bar-while-I-was-crying-on-a-train-in-2009 to step forwards and say a few words. I'd like someone to give *her* a Mars bar.

Finally, I'd like the barmaid I used to say hello to at that vegan place to get up and read a poem. Something by R. D. Laing, about the fraught, fucked-up nature of human relationships. Something about schizophrenia. Something about the relationship between schizophrenia and death.

Once that awful, grinding, coffin-on-a-conveyor-belt noise is over and done with, and my choice of song blares out of the speakers (that tune from the closing credits of *Porridge*) I'd like everyone to dance out of the room and head to the wake.

And that's where the real fun will begin.

I want the wake to be held at the house where I grew up. I know there's a new family living there now, and it might inconvenient for them, but if they wouldn't mind giving up their home for this one last favour, then I'd be much obliged. I did live under that roof for twenty-four years, after all. Had my first orgasm there. Played my last game of *Pass the Pigs*.

So. Here's how it will be done. I'd like everyone to gather in the kitchen, where cheese and onion sandwiches and cava will be served, and maybe the odd pork pie, just like when my dad died.

I want the Top 25 'most played' list on my iTunes to be put on, and I want everyone to clap along to the music, only to lose the rhythm several bars in, and cross their arms in embarrassment. I want an Ethiopian woman I have never met to jump up and down and start ululating beside the Aga, in the very spot I used to sit, back when I was ten years old and scared.

In the living room, I want a suitcase full of memories to sit on the coffee table. The suitcase will hold a collection of short stories I wrote when I was eight, that pink bobble hat with a bunny rabbit on it, a razor blade, and the *Ha Ha Bonk* joke book. The razor blade will be caked in blood.

Though I encourage my guests to chat freely, I would like to impose a few guidelines. For example, I want my best friend from school and my best friend from now to sit at opposite ends of the house. They will not get on.

And I'm adamant that people talk about my bad points as well as my good. How stubborn I was. How unreliable, melodramatic. How controlling. I want people to cry when they hear the word 'controlling'.

I want the one man I have ever loved enough to spend my life with to be there too.

I want him to leave his new girlfriend at home and come out especially for me. I want him to play a song about my eyes, to play a song about our first kiss, a song about the best sex we ever had. I want him to tell everyone that *he* broke up with me.

I want there to be a moment, just one short moment, where he looks off into the middle-distance and says how special I was to him. How special I still am.

I want him to leave early.

As the party progresses, I'd like new things to happen.

I want all the people who ever got pissed off with me to gather in my old bedroom and throw darts at a picture of my face. I want the girl who told me I was a 'fucking bitch' to hit me right between the eyes.

I want my regrets to be exhibited as *objets d'art*, scattered around the front lawn and scorned by critics. The accidental threesome. The septic belly-button piercing. The accidental foursome. The two-day hangover. Chlamydia.

I want the man-who-made-me-get-down-on-my-knees-and-beg-when-I-was-thirteen to read out excerpts of my poetry from around that time, while everyone laughs at how wrong in the head I was.

Then I want that version of Pachelbel's Canon in D – *minor* – that I heard on YouTube to play as someone sets fire to a pile of all the words I ever wrote. I want the flames to devour each syllable as everyone cheers.

I want fireworks.

Once it's dark, I'd like things to get a little out of hand. I'd like everyone to run around naked on the driveway, as I did aged fifteen. To get drunk and emotional. To have fist-fights and cheat on one another. To experience blackouts and vomiting and concussion and tears.

To stroke each other's hair and tell each other it'll all be okay.

And I want my mum.

And stars to shoot out of the sky.

And I want my mum.

And my dad to come back from the dead, to sing that song about brushing my teeth, the one he sang every night before bed.

And my sister to stop being poorly, to leave the psychiatric hospital, be okay, be happy.

And I want my mum.

I'd also be grateful if – five minutes after my wake is over – the world was to end.

Nothing extravagant. Just one tiny apocalypse.

I don't need four giant horses to ride in, another world war to take place, or a sudden outbreak of zombies. Nothing that showy. Just a quick, discreet imploding. A quiet conclusion.

Because when I die, I don't want anyone to feel lost without me. In fact, I don't want anyone to feel anything.

These Little Rituals

We're not so different, you and I. We like to think we are, but we're not. You with your Y chromosome, your love of music, of God. And me with my books and my atheism and my cunt.

I'm the one that buys the erotica. The ancient pictures of men upon men, tangled together and screwing, a snarl of flesh and lust.

You're the one that buys the muesli. The expensive stuff, imported from Dorset, with berries and nuts and spelt.

I'm the one that cradles your head. Tells you you're clever when you lose faith in yourself. Gives you blowjobs when you're feeling blue. Shows you the pictures of the men upon men, tells you the history of sodomy in literature, asks if you're sure you're straight, if you're sure you want me.

And you're the one that says yes. Yes, I do love you. Yes, I will go and buy some more muesli. Yes, I do think the world is a strange place for people like you and me.

'What's it like to have breasts?' you ask me one night, while we stand with our backs to the wall, looking into the mirror, watching our breath on the glass.

'It's like having a swelling,' I tell you. 'When you sprain

your leg and your calf fills with fluid, and you just want to sit and massage it until the swelling goes down, until it drains away.'

'It won't drain away,' you say.

'It's draining,' I reply. 'But just very, very slowly.'

During the day, you go to the office. You switch on the radio and make sure the levels are right, that the cross-faders are used properly, that the interviews can be heard. It is a job of national importance, you tell me once in a while, and I nod and cradle your head, and ask you when you think the problems in Syria will end.

And during the day, I read my books. Not just the ones with dirty pictures, but also the classics: Dickens, Eliot, Austen, Scott. I write notes on them, rearrange their order on my shelf, move them back again.

'What's it like to have a penis?' I ask one morning, before you leave for work.

You undo your dressing gown, and I see it there, bobbing, harmless, impossibly small. 'It's like having an extra hand,' you tell me. 'Except the hand gets pins and needles in it, pins and needles so bad you can't actually feel the skin any more, just the red-hot tingling sensation, the vital sensitivity of it.'

'Can I touch?' I ask, stepping forwards.

'It doesn't feel like that right now,' you say. 'Now, it feels like nothing.'

Sometimes, when you're out, I like to play a game with myself. I like to push my stomach out as far as it will go, and run my hands over it, imagining there's a foetus inside, squirming and kicking and sucking its thumb, until the thought of it turns me on, and before long I'm getting off on it, pushing my stomach out, repeating 'baby, baby, baby, baby'.

When you're at work you like to collect post-it-notes. You've collected over fifty packs, in greens, pinks, yellows and blues. I keep asking you to bring some home for me, some heart-shaped ones maybe, but I've never seen a single one, and sometimes that thought makes me afraid.

'What about your cunt?' you ask at the dinner table. 'What does that feel like?'

I push the scallops around my plate for a while, then say: 'It feels like a balloon. A balloon that needs blowing up, a balloon that keeps losing air, a balloon with a leak, a balloon on a gate that is pointing out a party.'

'I like that one,' you tell me, sipping your wine. 'Yes, that one is good.'

We play together like this, you and I, every day and night, pretending we are living separate lives, pretending there is mystery when there's not. Because the truth is, we're the same, I and you. Exactly the same, with your cock and my cunt, my balloon and your post-it-notes. We're lovers who spend all our time with one another, in our minds if not our bodies.

When we do make love, although it's rare, we are no

longer fascinated by one another. I know how your dick feels better than I know my own fingers. You know each crease in my vagina better than you know the aisles of the supermarket.

But when you've had a bad day, or when I have, or both, then it works for us, asking these questions. Performing these little rituals. Pretending to be different, pretending that we want to know more. It makes us feel safe, and scared, and alive.

And to be perfectly honest, if you were to ever stop asking me about my breasts, or if you ever actually brought me a post-it-note home from your desk, or told me that you didn't believe in God any more, that He had deserted you, then that's when I'd know, there was nothing left between us, there was no hope for either of us any more.

Vegetables And Nietzches

I was radical. I was vegan.

I was a punk-rocking pink-haired pierced-tongued head-banging vegan. And to prove just how radical and vegan I was, I joined a commune.

Well, I say commune.

Really, it was a four-bedroom semi-detached house in Lenton: the student area of Nottingham. But, just like any other commune, it was bound by belief. Belief and rules. I mean, not *rule* rules, just rules. Like, we had a pot for receipts, shopping bags made of hemp, a cooking rota, etc.

Out of the four of us, I was the only girl. For some reason, I was also the only one that honestly, truly, adhered to the rules. But then I guess I was the one that put the receipts pot on the windowsill, hung the hemp bags on the back of the cupboard, and stuck the rota to the fridge. I suppose I was hoping to lead by example. Not that we had a leader, of course. That's not how a commune works.

So, there was me, the only girl, and then there were three others: Danny, Tom and Rex.

Danny was the most intense. The commune was his idea, and it was driven by strong political principles. Principles like: *let's have a revolution!* And: *down with taxis!* Yeah, that's right. Taxis. Bad for the environment, apparently. To save the environment, Danny said, we needed to start our own rickshaw service. We'd transport members of the public to and from the Sainsbury's down the road, and we'd do this for free. Think of the difference it would make! We would make!

Danny referred to us as the *vegan warriors*. Everything he owned fitted into one suitcase. He was so radical that he didn't wash. The body cleans itself, he said. The body is amazing. Animals are amazing. Plants are amazing. Rickshaws are amazing. Danny was a nice guy but he smelt terrible.

Next there was Tom. Tom was quiet and bookish. He'd been vegan for longer than the rest of us combined. He worked in the university library, and we knew him the least. Tom was straight edge; no meat, no dairy, no booze, no sex. We were all scared of Tom. We worshipped him. We had nothing whatsoever to say to him.

And then there was Rex. Rex was everything you'd expect someone called Rex to be. He had chiselled features, a razor-sharp jawline, sun-kissed skin, and long blond dreadlocks. He was desperately smart, desperately witty, and desperately handsome. He was also desperately *not* vegan, but we bent the rules for him every time. Besides, he was only staying with us for the summer. After that it would be the vegan core remaining. The vegan hardcore.

So what about me then? Where did I fit into all of this?

Well, I'd been vegan for almost a year. It started just before I moved into a house with three other girls. The girls were all vegetarian. We had laughed about it before we signed on the dotted line. We'll never have to clean pig fat from the grill! Never gag at the sight of bloody meat in the fridge! Never be tempted to abandon our morals due to the delicious, tantalising smell of bacon! Mmm, bacon.

Actually, I was the 'least vegetarian' of them all, as I'd

only recently stopped being a militant meat-eater. Growing up on a smallholding and eating your own animals kind of makes you that way. Our animals all had names. In a sense, I ate my pets. Rosie and Jim with gravy and peas. Frisky with garlic butter. Mint-Choc-Chick, battered with chips.

But I guess my move to vegetarianism, then veganism, happened because of all that. Aged seventeen, with a forearm of scars and a shelf of Marilyn Manson CDs, I needed to rebel. Vegetarianism was a sure-fire way to piss off my parents, but then, when I got to uni, that wasn't enough. Vegetarians were everywhere. Veganism was special.

So I informed my housemates-to-be that I was now off dairy. My meals would need to be kept in a separate part of the fridge. Segregated.

If only I'd kept *myself* segregated, like my food. In the first week, I made the fatal error of getting it on with one of my housemates, Theresa. After that, on occasion, I would sneak into her room in the middle of the night and we'd kiss, long and hard, then she'd tell me about which boy she was seeing at the moment, and whether or not she was going to have sex with him.

Inevitably, this arrangement made me very lonely. It involved going behind the other housemates' backs, and eventually, after a tiff with Theresa – a really stupid tiff about a phone bill – I barely said a word to any of them.

The commune was a new start.

I knew it was going to take something big. Something radical.

I'd been living at the vegan house for almost a fortnight,

and was walking back there from campus. I'd just handed in my last essay of the semester, on R. K. Narayan's *The Man-Eater of Malgudi*. The book was okay, fairly readable, but there was a great bit at the end. This character called Vasu, a strong but self-centred taxidermist, feels a mosquito on his temple and swats it away, but in doing so, damages a nerve in his head. Bang. Instant death. I've always liked things like that. The weird ways that people die.

As I walked home that day, thinking about this scene from the book made me very aware of my own body. It felt bulbous and wrong. The elasticated band of my knickers cut into my hips. My bra strap, which was a 32C but should really have been a 34B, clawed at my back. My jeans made a daft noise when they rubbed together at my thighs. Swoosh swoosh. It was the sort of noise that should have been in a cartoon.

I felt strangely relieved when I reached the house. 'Hello!' I called, opening the front door.

I took off my satchel, and put it on the mat. Listened.

Then I stripped off.

First the coat, then my top, jeans, socks, bra, pants.

Even though it was June, and sunny outside, I was surprised how cool it was, standing there at the front door, naked. I looked down at myself, at the impressions left by my clothes. The toothlike ridges from the top of my socks. The two dents, like a scowl, from the underwire between my breasts.

Stepping over my clothes, I walked into the kitchen. *Check it out*, I thought. *I'm naked. I'm naked in the kitchen.* I lifted a dirty pan, still on the hob from last night. The remains of Danny's kidney bean pasta. His philosophy was that as long as the basic nutrients are there it doesn't really matter about the taste. I put the pan in the sink. It had been Rex's turn to do the washing up. None of us had the heart to reproach him for not doing it. Not when he had a jawline like that.

There was a rustle behind me.

'Oh, Tom, fuck! I didn't realise anyone was at home!' My hands sprung to my breasts. Crotch. Breasts. I stepped forwards and hid my pubic hair behind the microwave.

Tom smiled, then hid his smile behind his book. He was reading Nietzsche's *Beyond Good and Evil*.

'Bloody nice day today, isn't it?' I said. 'I'm warm as toast. So you've probably noticed I'm not wearing anything. Is that a good book? I've never read any Nietzsche.'

Tom put the book on his lap. 'It's very good,' he said gently.

'So the thing is…'

At that moment the front door opened. It was Danny.

'Hey guys,' he said, stepping over my clothes and taking an apple off the sideboard, his gaze fixed on the barbell in my left nipple.

'Right,' I sighed. 'Well I may as well tell you both at the same time.' I felt a surge of courage and let my hands fall to my sides. 'I've decided not to wear clothes for a while. When I'm in the house. I hope that's okay.'

Danny took a bite of his apple, then said: 'Fine by me.' A lump of white mush shot out of his mouth and onto the linoleum.

I looked at Tom. He bowed his head and went back to his book.

That night, in an effort to show Danny that just because

we were vegan it did not mean we had to ignore our taste buds, I cooked up something ambitious. Roasted aubergine stuffed with macaroni-Sheese and breadcrumbs. It was a bit awkward, cooking with no clothes on, not just because of the grease and the heat, but also because of Danny's stare. But fuck it, I was radical. I was vegan.

Just as we'd taken our plates over to the sofa, Rex and his girlfriend walked in.

Rex's girlfriend, Indya, was absolutely perfect for him. She had long blonde hair and sun-kissed skin, like he did, but she was different too. She had such dainty features, these big green eyes and dark pink lips. They walked into the living room with their arms around one another, smiling with their straight, white teeth. When they caught sight of me, their arms untwined.

'Wow,' said Indya. 'Is this a statement? Is it a vegan thing?' Indya, like Rex, was vegetarian, and somewhat in awe of our decision to cut out dairy. I couldn't help but feel that her green eyes were fixed on the hair between my plate and my navel.

'She's renounced clothes,' said Danny, taking a mouthful of Sheese and grimacing.

'I felt uncomfortable with them on,' I explained.

Indya took a step closer, still eyeing my pubes. 'That's so cool!' she laughed. 'Can I join in?' Without waiting for an answer, she grabbed a blanket off the sofa, wrapped herself in it, and undressed.

'Any food left?' asked Rex, opening the oven door.

'Loads,' I said, deflated. 'It's disgusting.'

'Sheese tastes like socks,' Tom added, then dived back into the safety of Nietzsche.

Indya, now naked except for the blanket, sat on the sofa

beside me. 'Feel free to snuggle up if you get cold,' she said. Then, with an element of concern, she whispered: 'I've left my knickers on. I'm not as brave as you.'

That evening, Indya and I sat in my room while the boys were outside learning to juggle with Danny's new clubs. Every now and then, laughter erupted and we'd hear one of them clapping or swearing, and I feared it'd only be a matter of time before we heard a window smash or someone get hurt.

Being naked, albeit under a blanket, seemed to have had quite an effect on Indya. I knew how she felt. I was becoming more confident in my own skin too, like the time I gave up drinking for three months and became a really good dancer. Now that there were no imprints left behind from my underwear, and there was nothing to cut or dig or chafe, I felt pretty good. Like my body was meant to be the shape it was, and there were no ill-fitting clothes to tell me otherwise.

'Rex and I have been doing all sorts of amazing things lately,' Indya said, running her hand over my duvet cover. 'Last week, for my birthday, he bought me champagne and strawberries.' She wriggled a little closer and put her hand to her mouth. 'He dipped the strawberries inside me and then sucked off the juice. It was so romantic.'

I was sitting on the bed cross-legged, and pushed my heel gently against myself. I could feel my own wetness on the dry skin of my heel. I wished someone would dip strawberries into me.

'He gives me the most amazing orgasms,' she sighed.

I took my heel away and rubbed it on the duvet. 'Indya,'

I asked slowly, 'how do you have an orgasm?'

We looked into each other's eyes and heard a window smash.

Indya came back to the house the next day. She took off all her clothes, except for her bra and knickers, the moment she entered my room.

'Look,' she said, handing me a vibrator. It was very plain: a thick silver stick with one speed setting. It was the first vibrator I had ever held. Lighter than I'd imagined one to be. And colder. 'Simple, but it does the trick,' she giggled. 'Use it as much as you like. Just give it a wash afterwards.'

That night, I held the vibrator deep inside myself, listening to the dull buzz and wondering how it would feel to kiss Indya.

The nakedness grew boring. My breasts felt like they were starting to droop, I got my period and had to put a tampon in, and I became more aware of being inside my skin than ever before. The liberation I felt when I enclosed myself in a bra and pants was unbelievable.

Fully-clothed, I headed out to a gig with Indya and Rex.

They walked either side of me, in their beautiful clothes. Rex's shirt was embroidered with kingfishers. Indya was in a floor-length skirt and lace-trimmed vest, with red and gold bangles going halfway up her arms. I wore jeans and a t-shirt. I'd given myself a haircut and my faded pink hair was gelled into two-inch spikes. We walked up the hill towards the town centre, in the evening sunshine. None of us had said anything for the past few minutes, but now Rex spoke. 'Indya and I have something to ask you, don't we, honey?'

I looked at the dimple in the centre of his chin; imagined Indya's tongue pushing into it, making him groan. Oh, to be that tongue.

'We'd really like to have a threesome with you,' he said. 'What do you think?'

I put my hands into my pockets and took them out again. 'Well,' I stammered. 'Okay, yes, of course I'll do it.'

After the gig, Indya went back to her house to do some revision, and I stayed up in Rex's room, listening to The Smiths and talking about what book Rex was reading at the moment and how his History Degree was going and his favourite films and anything he wanted to talk about really.

I was perched on the laundry basket in the corner, sipping a generous helping of Isle of Jura ten-year-old single malt whisky from a mug. 'I really liked that last song they played tonight,' I said, taking another sip of whisky, wishing I had some water to dilute it with.

'Yeah? I thought that one was a bit, I don't know, gimmicky.'

'Maybe you're right,' I said. 'You're probably right.'

Rex threw back the rest of his whisky and looked me square in the eye. 'I'm looking forward to the threesome,' he said. The moment the words came out, the track on his stereo ended, and we sat there, staring at each other. And then The Smiths again.

Girlfriend in a coma...

Rex touched the space on the bed beside him. 'We should get some practice in beforehand.'

Those wide, sincere eyes.

'We don't want to mess up, do we?'

I went over to his bed and let him undress me.

'That's right,' he murmured. 'Nice tits. Nice pussy.'

He took the bottle off his desk and poured whisky onto my neck and my breasts. Then, sitting over me, he poured it onto himself. 'Lick it off,' he ordered.

He took a huge mouthful of whisky and then a mouthful of me, and within a few moments we were having sex, stinging.

The next day I hung out with Indya. Rex was at uni. Evidently he hadn't said anything and I wasn't about to either.

Indya and I sat on the bed, listening to The Mad Caddies. I gave her back the vibrator.

'What did you think?' she asked.

'Great,' I told her, thinking how much better her boyfriend's penis had been inside me the night before.

'Did you have an orgasm?' she asked.

'Yeah,' I lied, wondering if I would ever have one.

She wrapped the vibrator in a few sheets of toilet roll, then inside a plastic bag, and put it in her handbag. 'I've never been with a girl,' she said. 'I'd love to kiss you.'

I didn't stop to discuss it; I pushed her onto the pillow and we kissed. I pulled down her skirt and kissed her French knickers. Pink, with a white bow and trim. La

Senza, if I wasn't mistaken.

Sitting over her, as Rex had done over me, I took off my Dead Kennedys t-shirt, and let Indya unbutton my jeans. We squirmed and sucked and nibbled, and eventually, we undid each other's bras. I ran my pierced nipples over hers and shivered. I told her how lovely she was and pulled at her pants. 'Not until the threesome,' she said quietly.

Neither Rex nor Indya had mentioned the threesome in over a week, and I was beginning to think it would never happen.

Rex and I fucked three more times. Each time it was at his suggestion of 'getting in the practice', and each time it involved whisky. I noticed that when the Isle of Jura ran out it was replaced with Sainsbury's own brand, and, though it tasted worse, it stung less. I wondered if he and Indya used whisky too. It was difficult to get the smell out of my hair. I began to wear perfume to mask it.

For every fuck I had with Rex, I had an encounter with Indya. She'd let me pull at her pants with my teeth until I could touch her hair with my tongue, soft and blonde and wonderful, but I still wasn't allowed to taste her.

Today, though, I was going to go for it. She was due round in half an hour, and I planned to kiss her into such a frenzy that when I whipped down her pants, she'd be too worked up to say stop. It's not a plan I'm proud of.

I had a bath, lit some scented candles, put on some nice underwear, perfume, a little more perfume, and beside my bed, I placed a punnet of strawberries.

As I waited for her to arrive, I danced around the room to Rancid's ...*And Out Come the Wolves*, thinking about how great it was to be young right then, at that moment in time, and how terrifying it was going to be to get old.

There was a knock at the door. It was Rex.

'Rex. I thought you were out all afternoon.'

'You look sexy.'

'Thanks.'

'Can I come in?'

'I guess. Is it okay if I just make a quick phone call?'

Rex shut the door behind him. 'Sure, I'll just stand here. Amuse myself.' He unzipped his trousers.

'Christ, Rex. I'm a bit busy today.'

'You going somewhere?'

No, I–' The phone call wasn't an option, so I sent a hurried text.

SHiT. REX HeRE!

As soon as I hit send, the doorbell went. 'Fuck, I think that might be Indya,' I said.

'Don't worry, she's at work.'

'No, she texted me earlier. Her shift was cancelled.' I could hear her downstairs, talking to Tom.

'Fuck.' Rex shoved himself back into his trousers. I spotted the bulge in his jeans as he went out of the door. 'Honey, so good to see you,' he called, and his bedroom door slammed shut.

I switched off my music and stood by the door, breathing heavily. I heard the squeak of a mattress. The bang of a headboard. A gasp, a whimper.

I looked at myself in my wardrobe mirror.

It was obvious when I saw myself now. Stupid underwear. Stupid hair. Stupid piercings. I wasn't a woman; I was a statement.

I sat on the floor and ate strawberries until my fingers were stained red.

The next day we were in the living room having dinner: me, Tom, Danny and Rex. Tom had microwaved one of his mum's frozen shepherd's pies. She brought them to the house every few weeks, dozens and dozens of tinfoil containers of vegan shepherd's pie – no wonder the guy had never learnt how to cook.

We were having a House Meeting. Danny had discovered that although we'd gone to such great lengths, us vegan warriors, to maintain our commune in the most moral and perfect and brilliant way possible, using vegan bacon, vegan shoes, and even vegan toothpaste, we now had an enormous problem.

Our tap water wasn't vegan.

It was filtered, so he told us, using animal bones.

'I say we stage a protest,' he said, with a mouthful of pie, 'outside the waterworks.'

Tom didn't look happy. 'But in the meantime,' he asked, 'what are we going to do about the water situation? We need to drink. Wash.'

'We'll have to buy bottled water,' Danny replied. 'If we get this rickshaw thing set up, we can cycle back at least a dozen containers in one go.'

I put my empty plate on the carpet. 'Isn't that worse for the environment? I mean, we're vegan because we care about the environment, right?'

Danny snorted. 'Well, it's a little more complex than that.'

'Surely buying a load of plastic water bottles from Sainsbury's is far worse than using our own tap water, even if it's been filtered using the odd bone or two?'

Danny's eyes moved down to my chest. Even though it was covered in a bra, t-shirt *and* jumper, I felt him staring at my left nipple, like he had done that day at the start of summer.

'Look,' said Tom, 'we need to stick to our principles.'

Danny smiled at Tom's use of the word principle.

Rex put his empty plate on top of mine. 'Guys,' he said, 'I'm staying out of this one.' And he left the room.

A fly buzzed behind my head. Something was welling up inside me. Was it the heat? Tom's mum's shepherd's pie? Was I going to be sick? No. It was a different feeling. It was anger.

'Let's think of some witty slogans,' suggested Danny.

This anger – yes, it *was* anger – it was a new feeling. Or at least, an old feeling, but one I hadn't felt for ages. Christ, I thought this feeling was history now that I'd become vegan. That's what this commune was all about, wasn't it? No meat, no dairy, no anger.

My fists were clenched. I felt the muscles in my face grow tight, and a soft tickle on my cheek.

A fly.

Without thinking, I bashed my face, felt a crackle down my left cheekbone, and then pulled my hand away so see two black spindly legs stuck to the knuckle.

Danny and Tom opened their mouths.

I stood up. Tried to say something, but nothing came out. Danny and Tom kept their eyes fixed on my cheek. I lifted my hand to my face and brushed off the fly's remains. It fell onto the empty plate by my foot.

Tom coughed.

I walked over to the kitchen, grabbed a bin bag from under the sink, and then went upstairs. Rex was in his room, laughing and saying 'honey'. I went into my room.

There, I opened the bin bag and threw in every single item of clothing I owned.

I walked back downstairs, carrying my clothes, and marched out of the house, my eyes fixed on the Cancer Research shop at the end of the street.

So this was it. I was beyond it all now. Beyond Nietzsche, beyond aubergines, beyond good and evil.

What I really fancied, more than anything, at that very moment, was a big slab of meat and a glass of milk. Then after that – well, who knew? Maybe a trip to the nearest letting agent, maybe another piercing, maybe a vow of chastity, maybe a revolution.

Like Runner Beans, Like Electricity

When Curly Watts named a star after Raquel on *Coronation Street* in 1994, Mum cried. 'I think that's the most romantic thing in the world,' she said.

The next Christmas, Dad named a star after her. She didn't cry, but said she liked it infinitely better than the dishwasher he'd bought her the year before.

In *Coronation Street*, shortly after Raquel saw the star, she confessed that she didn't love Curly, that she was still in love with her ex. Curly flew into a heartbroken rage, and vandalised the shop where he worked, which promptly got him the sack.

Dad set up a telescope in the bedroom and laid out the chart with the position of Mum's star marked on it. They spent an evening finding it, looking at it, and then the telescope stayed by the bedroom window for several months, gathering dust.

When you live in the countryside, you can see the stars really well. I used to stand on the driveway at night, after long car journeys, and spin around, head to the sky, looking up at it all, until Mum called me indoors.

I was good at recognising the Plough – that one was easy – and usually Orion's Belt too, but the rest were a mystery. I quite liked it that way to be honest. It made me scared to think that every single star in the sky might have a name, that human beings might run out of things left to quantify.

Dad knew far more constellations than me. His first proper job, which he did after his PhD, was for the European Space Agency in Germany. That's where I was born, and why I was given a German name, as a souvenir from the trip. At the Space Agency, Dad designed the image processing software for satellites. We still have some of the original colour photographs that his satellites took of the Earth from space. I have one framed on my wall, marked *25 March 1982*, showing our planet exactly as it looked when I was a four-month-old foetus.

It's strange to think that my dad, who dedicated his life to such up-to-the-minute technology, chose to move to a hamlet in rural Buckinghamshire – so remote it couldn't even get a decent internet speed.

The only time I really, truly understood what connected him to that place was when I looked up into the night sky, twinkling like the room full of computer servers at the back of his office. I could almost see the wires, coming down from the stars and plugging themselves directly into our back garden. That sky was for my dad, for us.

Memories sparkle.

I'm five years old, running after Holly, laughing. Holly is our dog, a collie, and it's her job to guide the sheep around the paddocks. We have Soay sheep, a rare breed hailing from a remote island in St. Kilda.

'Don't chase Holly,' Daddy says. 'She's working.'

'Can I catch a sheep?' I ask.

'You can stroke one,' he replies. 'Want to do that?'

Once the sheep have been herded to the end paddock, Holly bounds off back to the house to play with Mum, and Daddy and I sit on the grass. We touch the sheep's fleece, which is tougher than you'd expect it to be.

How does that work, Daddy?

'Soay sheep were probably the earliest form of domesticated sheep kept in Europe. Dating back to the Neolithic period.'

People laugh at my dad because he tells me so many things I don't understand yet. When I was a baby he would walk me around the house, whispering into my ear about how the gadgets in every room worked, how light switches were made, how filaments in the kettle heated water to make a cup of tea.

I like hearing Daddy talk science. There's nothing he doesn't know the answer to. Like: why is the sky blue? Where do rainbows come from? If people had wings, could they fly? He has the answer to everything. In fact, he has such long, detailed answers, that I listen to his responses like songs, letting them wash over me, enjoying their soothing sounds, but never truly grasping the words.

'Look how cute Trevor looks today,' Dad says with a sudden laugh, and we watch Trevor chewing the grass, admiring his gentle eyes, and the soft fur on his face.

They are such small, intelligent creatures, these Soay sheep, nimble on their feet, with long, curved horns and inquisitive personalities. Also, their fleece moults naturally, so they don't need shearing. They're nothing like the fluffy, white, cloudlike creatures you see so often in the English countryside – many of our sheep are brown or grey, more like mountain goats.

I'm not sure why we ended up getting such rare sheep from such a remote part of Scotland. The fact that we live in an English hamlet, in a place with no bus stop, no local shop, not even a post box, feels remote enough to me. Even as a five-year-old, I feel we live on an island, a magical faraway Enid Blyton sort of place, and so I suppose, in a way, our strange sheep belong here too.

'Come on,' Daddy says after a while, 'let's go and do some gardening.'

I'm six, and I'm helping Dad in the vegetable patch. The car door is open, and Radio 4 is playing a Saturday Drama.

Daddy is in the greenhouse, cutting slots into grow-bags and putting in tomato plants. I always check on the plants on the way to school, having a quick peek in the greenhouse to see if the tiny green baubles have started to turn red yet, waiting impatiently for that first tomato of the summer, cut in half and dipped in salt.

I'm working in the herb garden. Lottie and I have our own section of the vegetable patch, half a square metre each, where we grow chives. Lottie doesn't like it when things die, but chives are hardy, and they grow interesting flowers, so we've planted lots of them.

I'm concentrating so hard that when Daddy calls me over, at first I don't hear. 'Greta!' he calls. 'Gret! Come and look at this.'

I put down my trowel and see Dad standing next to a pile of bamboo sticks.

How does that work, Daddy?

'I'm going to build a frame for the beans,' he says. 'Can you give me a hand?'

I open my fist and throw the flowers into the hedge. We set to work on this task together, very few words passing between the two of us, but every pause filled with love and wonder, and the thick, rich words of Radio 4 weaving themselves around us like runner beans.

I've had a bad dream. It's the worst nightmare I've ever had. I dreamed that Ronald McDonald was chasing me around the garden.

I get out of bed and tiptoe over to the window and look out. There's a big, crescent moon, and there are lots of stars in the sky. The garden looks peaceful. No sign of Ronald, but he might be hiding in the bushes, so I tiptoe downstairs and look for Mum and Dad. The living room light is on and Dad is still up. He's reading a book by Isaac Asimov, with a picture of a rocket on the front cover.

I walk in, rubbing my eyes and frowning, and Dad puts down his book. 'Greta!' he says. 'You're awake.' He pats his legs and I jump onto his knee and nestle my face into his neck.

'I had a nightmare,' I tell him, in a baby girl voice.

'Oh no,' he says. 'I thought we'd agreed you were going to dream about ice-cream tonight.' Every night, before I go to sleep, my dad sits on my bed and does times tables with me, then he asks me what I want to dream about, and he works his Daddy Magic and arranges for it to happen. One night I asked him what *he* wanted to dream about and he said ice-cream, so ever since I've decided that this is what *I* want to dream about too.

'Can I read one of your books?' I ask, picking up the Asimov and admiring the spacecraft on it, thinking how good an astronaut my dad would make.

'Course you can,' he says. 'Why don't you go over to the shelf and pick the one you'd like to read most?'

I run my hands along the lines of Terry Pratchett, Iain M. Banks, and Douglas Adams. 'I want this one,' I say finally, my finger resting on the smallest book on the shelf, a *Collins Gem Guide to Farming*.

'Are you sure?' Dad says. 'It's got a lot of technical stuff in it.'

I flick through the pages and see diagrams of slaughtered cows, pregnant sheep, and plucked chickens. 'Yes,' I say. 'This is the one.'

I take it to bed and read about cuts of beef for a while. Eventually I fall asleep, cuddling the book like a teddy bear.

I'm eight now and it's still the only thing I sleep with. I call it Farm Book. My sister has Raggy, Lulu, Cream Puff, and a whole host of other soft toys, which she lines up and bids sweet dreams to every night before bed, but for me, it's all about Farm Book.

Every Friday for Show and Tell, while the others in my class bring in toys they got for their birthday, or found in their cereal packets or Kinder Eggs, I bring Farm Book. I show my class a different page of the book every week, be it the chicken's digestive tract on p.161, the mating pigs on p.143, or the parasitic eggs on p.79, and the class listen politely. Then Alice or Jimmy will get up next and talk about their fluorescent green straw from Disneyland with Mickey Mouse's head on it, and Farm Book will go back in my bag for the day.

I'm amazed, to be honest, that week after week the teacher puts up with it, but then my mum works at the school too. She was my teacher for two years running, before this new, larger school was built. The old school was actually based on a farm. I don't remember much about going to school there, except that we stopped classes once because there was a thunderstorm so big that we were allowed to run over to the window and watch it. Once the number of pupils grew, the school moved to Milton Keynes, a 'new town' with much more glass than grass. Although our new school is next to an equestrian centre, and we sometimes go pony riding in the afternoons, we are no longer surrounded by nature. Perhaps, for the teacher, Farm Book and I are helping bridge that gap.

In fact, as the teacher's confidence grows, I am allowed to bring new things to Show and Tell. One week I bring some goslings, which my mum helps me carry in a cage, and Mum and I explain how hatching works. Another day, and this is the best, my entire class gets on a minibus, and we go on a school trip to my house.

Dad is waiting on the driveway with a clipboard. 'Welcome to Ivy Cottage!' he calls, handing us all a worksheet. 'I'm going to show you around the garden, explaining how things work. Some of the things I say will help you answer the questions on your sheet. If you get all the questions right, you get a prize.'

How does that work, Daddy?

He takes us around the garden, bit by bit, to the pond, the old beehives, the chicken coops, the paddocks. 'This is Frisky the lamb,' he says. 'We reared him with a bottle of milk, putting him on the bottom shelf of the Aga to warm up when he was poorly. We'll be eating him in a couple of weeks.'

71

Everyone shrieks.

Sometimes Daddy asks for my help, and I feel so proud. 'Pick up one of the chicks, Greta,' he says. 'Let the boys and girls stroke it. But you have to be ever so gentle. Like this. And don't touch their eyes.'

I pick up my favourite of the new batch of chicks: Mint-Choc-Chick. She does a poo on my hand. White and runny, a mixture of faeces and urea, just like I've read about in Farm Book.

When I wake up, I can't find Mum and Dad. I run around the house and then outside, shouting, but they're nowhere to be seen.

The garden's really quiet. Even though I'm ten now, I still get scared. There's an old caravan by the bonfire, with bullet holes in the side. I sometimes think a bad man lives in it, watching me, and I don't dare go in.

When I go past the chicken coops, I notice something creepy. I can't hear the chickens. I look in the hen houses. I see a few piles of feathers, but not one Rhode Island Red.

I go back to the house, calling my sister, telling her Mum and Dad are missing, and the chickens are gone too, and we sit in the kitchen, crying.

Twenty minutes later, Mum and Dad come home. 'We've been at the garden centre,' they say. 'Didn't think you'd be awake yet.' And then they tell us about the chickens, and how a fox got them in the night.

How does that work, Daddy?

Eleven years old and I'm nearly big enough for secondary

school. I want to go to the girls' grammar because it gets the best results on the league table, and I want to impress my dad. I'm going to get the best score possible on the twelve-plus exam, because Dad told me that I'm perfectly capable of getting top marks in everything if I put my mind to it.

Dad works from home now. Has his own IT company with three employees. I go to the back of the house, where his office is, and ask him how to become a good runner. I agreed to do the 800-metre race for school sports day, because no-one else in the class volunteered. Dad used to run for his county as a teenager, until he found cigarettes, booze, and my mum. 'Jog around the garden three times,' he advises me. 'Do it every day until the race.'

So I go out into the long grass, which hasn't been mown in months, and I run through the empty paddocks, past the corrugated sheep house, which is starting to rust. I run past the pond, which froze over last winter and all the goldfish died, and I run past the chicken coops, never filled with chickens after the fox had its feast. I run as close to the caravan as I can without getting scared, then I slump on the driveway, out of breath.

I look at the vegetable patch in front of me, at the dandelions growing where once there were radishes, sprouts, and peas. And I wonder at what point it happened, this ending of childhood. Of Radio 4 dramas on a Saturday afternoon, of holding Daddy's hand and sitting on his lap and helping him make things grow and buzz.

I stare up at the sky and I can see the moon, even though it's still daytime. I remember the chatter of my classmates as they traipsed around this patch. I remember digging up four potatoes and picking some rosemary when we ate

Frisky for dinner. I remember the pant of the sheepdog. The chirp of the chicks.

I decide not to jog around the garden any more. It's like looking at my life through the wrong end of a telescope. Remembering how it was before we had to give away Holly because she kept running onto the road. Before Dad announced at the dinner table on Christmas Day that he had gone off poultry. Before Mum stopped making piccalilli and sloe gin, and began eating crisps and drinking wine out of a box. Before Dad spent four hours every night at the pub. Before Mum stopped smiling.

This is the moment, I think – watching the moon where the sun should be – this is the moment that the spark has gone.

After working at the Space Agency, making satellites that took pictures of stars, Dad designed one of the world's first graphical user interfaces. The most well-known graphical user interface is Windows for Microsoft. Dad didn't design that.

At one point, though, in the world of computers, he was a pretty big deal. He was on the front cover of *The Times*, dressed in a top hat and tails, beaming with pride. But while Windows did very well indeed, Dad's invention never journeyed far. I think he always felt he'd let himself, and us, down.

Ivy Cottage, our own slice of *The Good Life*, I realise now, was not a new beginning, but a last hurrah. The final attempt for Dad to make life perfect. To become self-sufficient. To be a star.

In his final years, Dad used to text me from his office at

home. *Just seen a fox in the garden*, he'd say. Or sometimes it was a deer, or a pheasant, or rabbit. A wild animal, seen through glass, while he sat inside, behind his screen.

That's great, I'd reply. *How are you?*

At the end of its lifetime, a star will contain some degenerate matter.

The smaller stars, once evolved, end up shrinking, often becoming white dwarfs and then fading away into nothingness, over a long stretch of time.

The larger stars, however, do not shed their layers like the small ones. They keep fusing and growing, fusing and growing, until they become so large that they can no longer support their own mass. Very powerfully, and very suddenly, they collapse at the centre, and this causes the rest of them to explode in a supernova. The spectacle is so bright that sometimes it can outshine a whole galaxy.

All that remains, when these largest stars have exploded, is a black hole.

How does that work, Daddy?

My dad would be able to explain this to you much better than me. He'd be able to tell you how it happened – and why – and he'd keep on telling you about it, explaining it and explaining it until you couldn't hear the words any more, you'd just feel the sounds moving around you, weaving in and out like runner beans, like wires, like electricity.

One Nothing Everything

All the pink had gone.

By the time I was sitting in the waiting room, I was grey. I'd been green a little earlier, and yellow before that, but now I was grey, and I needed to throw up.

It was the day after Boxing Day, which was also the day after the 2004 Indian Ocean tsunami. While, on the other side of the world, tectonic plates slipped and ruptured – displacing around 30 km³ of water, causing a set of waves with an equivalent energy to that of about 5 megatons of TNT, killing around 230,000 people – I had a ball of pus inside me, about the size of a cherry. Except nobody had spotted it yet.

It's amazing what fainting on the floor of A&E will do for you.

I was carried into a small room, and instructed to lie on the bed until the doctor arrived. I waited for the doctor, and I waited for my dad.

My boyfriend had brought me here. I had only seen him for a few hours when he made the decision. I'd been at home with my parents before that, shivering and sweating, but Mum told me to stop being so melodramatic, and Dad told me it was the flu. So they took me to my boyfriend's house, hoping I'd perk up, but when I got there, I ate a bit of leftover Christmas dinner, bent-double, then vomited. That was when the decision was made to bring me here.

When Dad arrived, he gave me a kiss and sat quietly in the corner.

The doctor felt my abdomen and my back, and I winced when he touched the left-hand side. 'If ten is the most painful pain you can ever imagine experiencing in your whole life,' he said, 'and zero is totally pain-free, where would you put yourself on the scale right now?'

It felt like there was a blade piercing my side. Or a beachball blowing up and up and up, about to explode inside me. But I couldn't quite think of a number.

I thought back to when my sister was little, that period when she went deaf, and her eardrums would perforate from time to time, the blood dripping down her neck while she screamed. I thought about my dad, who had dislocated his shoulders eleven times, the first while he was on a skiing trip with my mum, and the last while he chased a duck around the garden. And then I thought about a pain even more painful than that. I thought about the pain I felt in my head as I cut my own arm, far greater than the pain of the blade scoring the skin. I thought about the fires of hell. And torture chambers. And plane crashes and guillotines and red-hot pokers.

Eventually I told the doctor: six.

He gave me a cardboard bowl and told me to go and wee in it.

When I brought it back, warm and foul-smelling, I wondered whether the doctor was going to tell me I was pregnant. I hadn't had sex for several weeks – in fact, up until three days ago, I had been living in Berlin, completely alone. But there was always that chance. My boyfriend was in the waiting room outside, and there was always that chance.

'I'll be back in a minute,' said the doctor, after he'd dipped a bit of litmus paper into the urine.

My dad sat beside me and stroked my forehead. *I'm pregnant, Dad*, I thought, *and I don't think I want the baby. Not now, not yet. What should I do?*

The doctor came back with a nurse. 'You've got blood in your urine, as well as a lot of debris. We're going to get you in for an immediate ultrasound.'

'Debris?' asked my dad, and he and the doctor talked while I was wheeled into a dark room.

A severe-looking woman rubbed jelly under my ribcage and rolled me over. 'It's a left-side renal abscess,' she declared, a few seconds later.

I was wheeled to the urology ward, where a needle was stuck in my hand. 'Saline solution,' explained a nurse. 'For dehydration.' 'Antibiotics,' said another, administering a second drip. Someone else brought me a plastic cup containing some red liquid. 'Oramorph. It'll take the pain away. Whenever you want more, just press this button.' I swallowed the liquid and watched my dad and my boyfriend walk towards me.

'Isn't life great?' they said to me. 'Everything's fine. The clouds are fluffy. I can see a bunny rabbit.' Or they might have said get well soon, or something to that effect. I was too doped up to tell.

The next few days passed in a morphine blur. Doctors and nurses streamed in and out, drips were replaced, elderly patients shrieked in the night, and forgot their own names in the morning. Dad drove an hour to visit me every evening, and Mum came most days too. My sister came once, but it made her too upset and she left.

One day, when my dad turned up, he told me I was

starting to look less grey.

'Can I go home soon?' I asked.

'No darling,' he said. 'You've still got no colour in your cheeks.'

'Can I go home when I'm pink then?'

'I'm afraid you've got to have an operation,' he replied.

I wanted to go home and wash my hair. I was sick of pissing in a cardboard bowl and carrying my drip around the ward with me, and I was even getting sick of the nurses' soothing voices and the inside of my own head.

Later that day, a consultant described the operation I needed. I would get a slit cut in my side, he said, then all the pus would be sucked out of the kidney, and I'd be sewn back up again. It was risky, but if I didn't have it, the abscess would burst and leak into the rest of my body, and I'd get peritonitis.

What the doctor didn't tell me, but told my parents, was that even with the operation, I only had a fifty per cent chance of living. That the abscess was growing so big it was stretching my kidney, blocking my gut, and every moment it was inside me was a moment I might expire.

That was on New Year's Eve. My boyfriend went to a club in London, and texted me at quarter to midnight. WISH U WERE HERE, the text said. WISH U WERE HERE, I was tempted to text back. At ten to midnight, the nurses started cheering, eating cake and singing songs, while all the patients on the urology ward, full of pus and debris, lay there and looked on, occasionally screaming or crapping themselves. It wasn't my favourite New Year's Eve. Conversely, I was so pumped up on morphine, it probably wasn't the worst.

New Year's Day, I had an enema. I hadn't taken

a shit since Christmas Eve, and it was getting really uncomfortable. When the warm water gushed out of my back passage, down into the toilet, I was terribly embarrassed at the noise it made, but dismayed to find that it didn't work.

A week after that, I was taken in an ambulance to a different hospital. They had a better procedure there, with a higher chance of survival. The surgeon looked at my kidney on an ultrasound, and told me the abscess was now the size of an orange. 'It's very rare,' he said, 'to get something like this at such a young age. Have you ever been to Asia?' I told him I had not, and he informed me that there was a bug in my urine that originated in the Far East.

I was injected with something that made my mouth taste of metal, then placed on my side, still awake, while the surgeon pushed a catheter into my skin, all the way into the kidney, where the contents of the abscess were sucked out and drained into a plastic bottle. I had a tube hanging out of me, with a plastic bottle attached, for the following week. Every now and then, the bottle would get replaced, and more gunk would come out. A pint and a half in total. It was revolting, and a little bit wonderful.

For several hours after the operation, it felt like my insides were made of broken glass. Every breath was wretched, but a yawn or sneeze was truly excruciating. Never mind the plane crashes or guillotines or red-hot pokers I had imagined when I was first admitted to hospital – *this* was a ten.

The day after the operation, I managed to shit. Which was a relief after a fortnight of hospital food, let me tell you. The colour began to reappear in my cheeks too, and I started to feel more alive again. I even tried having sex with my boyfriend in the hospital bathroom. I bent over the side of the bath, gripping the bottle hanging out of my left-hand side while he thrust at me a few times before losing his erection. Then he washed me down with a flannel and we returned to the ward, my backless nightgown flapping open to reveal my buttocks.

When my boyfriend left, after making me promise to never talk of the bathroom incident again, I called my dad and asked him to bring me a book on haiku.

I'm not sure why, but in the days after my operation, I felt a sudden desire to learn everything I could about this particular form of Japanese poetry. So I learnt about Buson, Bashô and Issa, and I read poems about mushrooms and graves and moonlight and blossom. I looked at the tree out of the hospital window and imagined it covered in pink petals.

As I pondered the transience of life, I wrote haiku about my imaginary blossom, about how quickly it bloomed then fell away. I drank three large bottles of water a day, draining out the badness, letting my kidney shrink back to its normal size, giving it a chance to start over.

It was around that time, while I was working on my hospital haiku, that I realised that if I had been alive fifty – or maybe even twenty – years ago, I would not have survived. In the nineteenth century, I would have been described as having 'consumption', and put into bed to slowly and painfully waste away, while the abscess swelled and ruptured, a tidal wave of pus.

unavoidable
a natural disaster
human tsunami

I had been through a fair bit that last year. I had finished my Degree at the start of summer. Had arrived back home and tried, and failed, to commit suicide. My sister had also tried, several times, with little more success. My parents argued constantly, over things that were inexplicable to us. My drink was spiked. I started, and gave up on, psychotherapy. I sold all my possessions and moved to Berlin. Only a month later – after four weeks of extraordinary loneliness, of calling my boyfriend and telling him I didn't know what I was doing, that even though I was back in my country of birth I'd never felt so foreign – I returned defeated. And then, just three days after coming back, I'd been admitted to hospital.

I wrote one hundred and seven haiku in total. I wrote about chrysanthemums and pine trees, dragonflies and cicadas, nandina bushes and sacred mountains. Some of these I'd only seen in pictures. As I penned the first word of my one-hundred-and-eighth poem ('everything'), I was told I could go home.

I held my dad's hand while we walked through the hospital's sliding doors, and I knew that, even though I had been saved, a part of me, still, had died.

At home, I hugged my sister and drank one glass of champagne and two pints of water. I donated ten pounds to the tsunami appeal, broke up with my boyfriend, and applied to do Masters courses in faraway places. When I was accepted by a Scottish university, I travelled north, for a visit in the springtime. The whole place was full of cherry blossom.

Your Alter Ego Does Not Exist

Masters students get intellectual tattoos: David Foster Wallace quotations and quills. We talk about weighty issues like the correct use of a semi-colon; we drink a lot of cheap wine.

We constantly discuss how little work we're doing, and bump into each other in the library all the time. We start up Arts and Social Sciences e-journals, and get spots again like teenagers. We become proprietary about certain rooms on campus, and notice how young the Freshers look: 'Oh my God, I can't believe they were born in 1991. *1991!* I was, like, having *wet dreams* in 1991.' We hug every time we see each other. We hug for dear life.

At the end of each day, we sit on our sofas, eating pasta and pesto, watching *X Factor*, thinking about how much we want to achieve, and wondering who else we could have been, if only we'd lived our lives differently.

Six months into my Masters, I bought a magazine. In the magazine there was a quiz. It was entitled: 'Who is your alter ego?' and you had to answer thirteen multiple choice questions: 'favourite colour', 'attitude towards death', etc. I took the questions seriously, as I always do, so I answered: 'green', 'terrified of dying', and so on, and when I totted up the score, the answer I got was this:

'You don't have an alter ego.'

I paced around my flat for a bit and had a serious think. I made some coffee and smoked an imaginary cigarette, and thought some more.

I continued to think for the rest of that week. I thought about it when I was at the supermarket, buying my weekly farmhouse loaf (it just felt so much more *me* than regular white sliced). I thought about it when I was running on the treadmill at the gym (trying to sculpt my body into a shape of impossible proportions). And I thought about it while lying in bed at night, listening to the trains screeching into Partick station (wondering how it would feel to throw myself in front of them and let them crush my bones). Finally, I vowed to take action. I typed 'alter ego' into Google and prepared to flex my intellectual muscles.

The first result was Wikipedia. At the top of the page was a picture of a man playing cards with himself, and next to that it said 'this article needs attention from an expert'. Being a little snobbish about these things, I skipped it.

The second result was completely different. It wasn't so much informative as interactive. Not a thirteen question quiz, like the one I'd done in the magazine, but this time a full-blown hi-tech life-simulation browser-game. Whatever that was.

Create your own personal alter ego, it said.

So I clicked on the link.

Imagine you are about to be born, it said. *Do you want to be male or female?*

How exciting! My cursor hovered over female. But why should my alter ego be the same sex as me? I'd always fantasised about what it would be like to be a man. Life seemed so much easier for men. Click.

Choose a name, the game ordered.

If I'd had free reign, I'd have gone with something like Rambo or Zeus. Sadly, this was multiple choice, so I went with Jake.

How do you want to be born? the game asked.

Peacefully, I clicked. Because regardless of how I might want my alter ego to turn out, who doesn't want a peaceful birth?

Your birth is so peaceful it is entirely unmemorable, said the game. *Your mother and father will find it difficult to recall anything about the day you were born when you are older, which may result in low self-esteem.*

I was taken to a page full of colourful icons, each containing a different, seemingly random image. I clicked on the first icon, which contained an eyeball.

There's a hand coming towards you. Do you: cry, bat it away, or make a cute gurgling noise?

Fuck it, I thought. This is my chance. I'm going to live out my wildest fucking fantasies, right here, right now. I'm going to create the most carefree rebel this world has ever seen. I'll look like an angel in comparison to this guy. I clicked bat it away.

This is not good, said the game. *You have inhibited the maternal bonding process. Not only will you have an awkward relationship with your own mother, but you will likely find it difficult to talk to all women from now on.*

Shit. I thumped the desk. I wanted my alter ego to have plenty of relationships with women. Way more relationships than I've ever had. Jake's meant to be the guy that gets all the chicks. I clicked on an icon containing a brain.

You have three building blocks in front of you. The first

time you try piling them on top of one another they tumble down. Do you try again?

Well I wasn't going to make the same mistake twice. I would at least let my alter ego develop a smidgen of sensitivity to his surroundings for now. So I clicked yes. Yes of course I'll try again.

Excellent building skills, lauded the game. *You will make a great labourer when you are older: remember this.*

Oh balls balls balls, I thought. I don't want my alter ego to become a labourer. I want him to become a rock star or a cigarette manufacturer or a bank robber or a right-wing politician. Something like that. Come on, I said to myself. Think like Jake from now on. WWJD? I clicked on an icon containing a swan.

You are hurting all over! the game warned. *Do you: cry, toss and turn, or go to sleep?*

Cry, I clicked. For heaven's sake cry. I'm not getting cot death. I'm just not.

This does not make sense, said the game. *Your birth was so peaceful that the programmers do not believe you would cry in this situation. Choose again.*

So I clicked toss and turn, and the game told me I'd develop a sickly cough for the rest of my life.

It was two weeks since my alter ego had been born. I was spending roughly eight hours a day online.

According to the game, Jake was a twenty-year-old dental student with a slight stutter and a penchant for sausage rolls. He'd had romantic encounters with three girls. The first, Bridget, had a tantrum because she thought Jake touched her bum (which, disappointingly, he didn't); the second, Lydia, let Jake lick her right breast after a day out at the Natural History Museum; and the third, Gaynor, unzipped Jake's flies but then told him that his sickly cough was so off-putting she couldn't carry on.

I swept aside the pile of unwashed dishes next to my computer, ignoring the rumble in my stomach which told me I'd eaten nothing but Super Noodles for the last three meals, and I logged on.

You have an exam tomorrow, warned the game, *and you haven't done an ounce of revision. Your housemates invite you to a strip-club. Do you go with them, or politely refuse and tell them you've got work to do?*

Go with them, I clicked, well aware I had uni work of my own that I should have been doing right now. Go the fuck with them, for fuck's sake.

You lose your virginity, said the game, *to a stripper named Delilah.*

Yes!

Sadly, Delilah gives you chlamydia and you fail your exam the next day. You drop out of dental school and become a labourer.

Okay, I thought, well at least now my alter ego has *edge.* He's contracted an STI and flunked uni. This was progress. But I had to go further. I clicked on an icon containing a heart.

Meet someone? it asks. *Or break up with someone?*

Meet someone, I clicked. I hadn't met anyone to break up with yet.

Do you want to go out with: Tina, Marie, or Consuela?

Consuela, I clicked. The dirty bitch.

Consuela has an attractiveness of 6/10, a shyness of 7/10, and a hypochondriac rating of 8/10, said the game. *Do you want an experience with her?*

Yes, I clicked. I want an experience. Give me a mother-fucking experience. So apparently we went ice-skating and had a nice time.

Eighteen days in. My alter ego spoke conversational French, liked going for quiet bike rides at the weekends, and his favourite TV programme was 'Never Mind The Buzzcocks'.

I, on the other hand, had stopped taking showers. I only ate meals that could be prepared in under three minutes, and I was developing bedsores. Because I was spending so much time at my computer screen, I began to go on night walks. I stalked the late bars; became friends with one-eyed Jimmy and Pillhead Brian, who was all gums and no teeth. I developed a limp due to the uncomfortable angle of my desk chair, and I was suddenly short-tempered with strangers. I had slept with three different men that week, and I'd stood at Partick station four times, looking down onto the train tracks and imagining. I'd even started buying white sliced instead of farmhouse loaf.

Early one morning – so early, in fact, that I hadn't gone to sleep yet – I stumbled into the living room in my underwear, unplugged the phone, had a mouthful of cheap wine, and switched on my monitor. This is it, I thought. It's now or never. I looked again at the question that had been sitting, untouched, since yesterday afternoon.

You've had a bad day at work, said the game. *Do you: put on your slippers and relax with your wife and three children, or put a gun to your head?*

I lit a cigarette, a real cigarette, a Marlboro Red, and

blew smoke over the screen.

It might have been my exhaustion, or the wine, or the fact I thought I had another STI brewing, but as I pressed the button, I saw my finger move in slow-motion.

Goodbye, Jake.

I looked down at my thigh, ran my fingers over the thick black lines of my biggest tattoo: a pair of wovles, standing either side of Tiw, the Anglo-Saxon god of hope and war. The ink had faded, but only a little.

Sprint

Nine Inch Nails played in my headphones as my feet thumped the conveyor belt. Just the right BPM to keep me going at 10K an hour, and just enough filth in the lyrics to fuel my adrenaline. Lines about the smell of sex and a desire for escape. *Violate* rhyming with *desecrate*. The alliteration of *fuck* and *feel* and *flawed*.

My face wobbled as I ran. The wall in front of me was covered in mirrors; I used to think this was for the narcissistic undergraduates, to watch their exquisite young bodies in action. But then I realised that mirrors made time go faster. Sure, there was the TV screen in the corner, but that usually played MTV or some such dross. It didn't mean much with the sound off anyway: just a load of idiots, grinding. Looking in the mirrors and observing the people in the room was fascinating.

There was the girl with blonde braids on the cross-trainer, who moved like she was at a techno rave, high on ecstasy. She was always here; grinning and sweating when I arrived, grinning and sweating when I left. Then there was the hairy guy on the rowing machine, with enormous shoulders and the most dynamic jaw I have ever seen. Every movement he made propelled his mouth into an enormous suck-and-blow, like he was performing a lewd act on the air.

And there was the woman in the corner. What was it

about her exactly? Well, her face didn't wobble for one. There was not one dimple of cellulite below her skimpy shorts. I imagined that if you were to lie in bed with those taut, tanned quadriceps wrapped around you, you would be as close to happy as you could ever be.

Today she was wearing a t-shirt with a slogan on the back: GOOD IS THE ENEMY OF GREAT. I'd stared at it for twenty minutes on the cross-trainer behind her before I started running.

Unfortunately, there was some cretin in neon trainers and a DayGlo vest on the treadmill beside hers. Normally I went for that spot. I liked to run in time with her. I would sneak a look at her dashboard and copy her speed. Right, left, right, left, we would go, in perfect synchronicity, as if we were taking part in a three-legged race.

Since I'd only been coming to the gym for around four months, it wasn't easy to keep up. 5K in twenty-five minutes was tough. I'd lost track of the number of times I'd suffered aching thighs for her sake.

I followed her out of the gym once. Staying a few paces behind, I crossed the road and waited outside the newsagents. She came out a few moments later with a pint of milk and a copy of *The Guardian*, then disappeared down Bank Street. I hung back a moment then went to buy milk and a paper of my own.

That night I took *The Guardian* to bed, touching the pages and reading the adverts, murmuring *good is the enemy of great, good is the enemy of great*, until I fell asleep.

We all had our reasons for going.

Going to the gym helped distract me from the

following questions: what the hell was I going to do after my Masters? Was I capable of being an adult? Why wasn't I feeling good yet? What did it mean to be 'well'? Would my sister ever stop trying to kill herself? Should I go back on the antidepressants? Why did I have this terrible sense of foreboding? This sense that I was about to lose everything? What was the terrible, unspeakable thing that had happened to me, that thing that gnawed away at me in the early hours of every morning? What had I done? What had been done to me? Going to the gym was never the answer, but it was *an* answer, so I came here whenever I felt bad. Which was every day, sometimes twice a day.

When I wasn't at the gym, I lifted weights beside the sofa, or ripped up toilet roll into pieces and let it fall like snow onto the carpet.

But every time I got on the treadmill I found I could run that little bit faster, for that little bit longer, and I somehow I felt I was getting further and further away from the inside of my own head. My muscles ached and stretched and swelled between each gym visit, and I started to think I was becoming invincible.

Rather than making notes on the theme of identity in Wordsworth and Coleridge's *Lyrical Ballads*, I made notes on calories burned and consumed instead. I recorded the number of sets, repetitions, and kilometres achieved each day. This was my poetry now.

Barbell Bench Press, Sets 3, Reps 15,
Barbell Front Raise, Sets 3, Reps 15,
Dumbbell Side Crunch, Sets 3, Reps 20,

Dumbbell Squat, Sets 3, Reps 15,
Hammer Curl, Sets 3, Reps 15,
Skull Crusher, Sets 3, Reps 10,
Step Back Lunge, Sets 3, Reps 15,
Running machine 10K,
Cross Trainer 5K,
Rowing 1K,
Rest

My metabolism was a furnace. Nothing I ate stayed on my bones. I went down to a size eight, then a six, then smaller. It was difficult to find clothes that flattered a skeleton.

'I'm a gazelle,' I told my friends, as they yawned.

One Tuesday morning, I arrived at the gym early. So early it hadn't even opened yet. I stood in the sleet outside, and waited. At about five to seven, a figure walked up Bank Street.

'Morning,' she said.

We stood looking at one another. We'd never spoken before. I needed to make this good.

'Hi,' I said, trembling. 'Shame about the sleet.'

She nodded and put on her headphones.

In the changing rooms, our bodies faced opposite directions. I took my time lacing my personalised trainers, filling my flask with water, going for my third wee of the morning, and then walked into the cardio room after her. As usual, she went to the treadmill in the corner, and, casually as possible, I took the machine beside her.

In the mirror, her eyes locked onto mine. I could practically hear the engine revving inside her.

She began to walk, only for a few seconds, then increased her speed to 9–, 11–, 12.5–, 13K an hour. I started at six, hesitated, then copied her.

After ten minutes, I felt like I was being stabbed in the abdomen. Fifteen, and I was going to puke.

I don't know how I did it, but somehow I managed to keep going for twenty-one minutes. *She* hadn't even broken out in a sweat. Not one damp patch tarnished her crisp t-shirt, which flaunted the phrase: YOU DON'T GET A SECOND CHANCE TO MAKE A FIRST IMPRESSION.

I spluttered, tripped over my personalised trainers, and switched off the machine.

The doctor told me to avoid exercise for six weeks. My calf muscles were torn, he said. I needed to warm up properly in the future. Take things at a steadier pace. Getting fit was a marathon, he said, not a sprint. Except when it was a sprint.

So I stayed at home and ripped up toilet roll.

Six weeks became seven, and then it was two months. I was terrified I wouldn't be able to run 1K any more, let alone ten. Going to the gym had been all about personal improvement. Beating last time's figures. Knocking off a second here, adding on a rep there. I couldn't bear the thought of starting all over again.

I put on two stone. Grew softer all over. Spent twenty pounds on the ingredients for one steak pie. Took five hours to cook it. Ten minutes to eat it.

The snow on the living room carpet grew ankle-deep.

When I finally built up the courage to return to the gym, I could barely get into my shorts. I ate a packet of chocolate buttons before I left the house for luck.

There was a new sign on the cardio room door. It said: NO BAGS ALLOWED.

The TV screen in the corner was playing an advert for sanitary towels.

I got on a treadmill and looked in the mirror. I was still the same person I was three months back. If anything, I looked healthier now. I had breasts and a figure. Sure, my face wobbled more than ever, and now my bum wobbled when I was being fucked from behind, but no-one had ever complained. In fact, men always seemed drawn to my arse. I was only human, after all. I was a wobbly-arsed fuckable human being.

I stretched and warmed up, then with a deep breath, pressed the green button.

I built up my pace slowly, very slowly, from a saunter to a walk, from a walk to a jog, and, after five minutes or so, I found myself running at 10K an hour, surprised at how easy it was. I quickened to eleven. Still fine.

It was at that moment that I glanced up at the TV, and saw the face of Jeremy Paxman. His face was on the screen for a long time. So long, in fact, that I assumed he was dead. This must be some sort of news item – an obituary, I thought, caused by Paxman's sudden demise.

I grabbed the side of the treadmill. There was an art to running and watching TV at the same time, and I still hadn't mastered it.

If Paxman was dead, it was the end of an era. I mean, he'd only be what – fifty, sixty at most? Too young. Way too young to die. Perhaps it was a heart attack. Those tense Newsnight interviews had to take their toll sooner or later. If not a heart attack, then maybe an angry interviewee posted something explosive through his letterbox one day. *Dear Jeremy, Thanks for verbally assaulting me in our interview last week. Yours Sincerely, BANG.*

It may have been an accident. One of those celebrity deaths that would be talked about for years to come. Swallowing a toothpick. Gored by a goat. Crushed by a bale of hay.

I turned the treadmill speed back down to ten.

Eventually, the camera panned out from Paxman's face to reveal a studio full of eager scholars, and the show began. *University Challenge*. So Paxman wasn't dead. The world as I knew it was not about to end just yet.

I looked away from the screen and back to the mirror. I was no gazelle any more, but I kind of liked the feeling of that extra layer of fat bouncing around me as I ran. It made me very aware of the space I was taking up in the universe, and strangely, for once I didn't feel guilty about that.

I decided not to listen to Nine Inch Nails today, and instead enjoyed the gentle hum of the machine, the pounding of my feet. The novelty of *University Challenge* playing on the TV. *University Challenge*!

When I reached two kilometres, the door opened and in she walked.

She took the machine beside me and fixed her eyes on mine. Her face was gaunt; cheekbones prominent. Her t-shirt bore the slogan: BE ALL THAT YOU CAN BE.

I watched her treadmill turn and her shoes begin to pound the belt, as she ran at eleven, twelve, thirteen, a full-on sprint.

But this time there was no revving inside me. Sure, she was running faster than I was, and there was no way I could ever catch up, but that was okay; I was just getting into a rhythm.

I stopped running away from my reflection, and began, very carefully, to run torwards it.

Doctors

Congratulations and hurray for you!

What you have achieved is no mean feat. It makes you kind of special. Heroic, even. Not only did you get your Masters, you wee genius, but you got a Distinction. That's right; with a capital 'D'. You can put MLitt at the end of your name now, if you want. You can show off about this for the rest of your life.

Thank goodness you didn't go to Paris to become a mime artist, like you said you would. Christ no, that Masters was definitely the right choice.

And by golly, you learnt so damn much. What did you learn again? You learnt that writing doesn't have to be like a million fireworks all going off at once. You learnt that you shouldn't try to illustrate your own work. You learnt that you have a distinctive and original voice. You learnt that having lunch with famous authors is overrated. And you learnt that it is possible to lose a condom inside yourself during a one night stand, only to find it two days later while doing a wee, oh horror, oh horror.

So what did you do after your Masters then, you whiz kid, you? Did you pen your great novel? Move abroad? Teach poor, sick children how to read and write? No, you did not. You took a full-time job in a card shop. At the card shop, you had to polish the front of every card in the shop, every morning.

After a week and a half, you began to miss uni. You were treated like a god at uni. You had lunch with Margaret Atwood at uni. You were never asked to polish the cards or count the novelty pencils at uni.

So on your day off you went back. Standing in the English Literature office, you told the course convenor you might like to do a PhD. When he asked why, you didn't mention Margaret Atwood or novelty pencils. You said: 'Because I want to be a Doctor, like my dad.' 'Okay,' he replied, 'that's as good a reason as any.' He handed you a thirty page application form with seventy-two pages of guidance notes, and then you polished cards and waited.

Sometime in late August, you received a letter saying your application had been successful. You were going to do a PhD. And what's more, you were going to be paid to do it.

The people at the card shop gave you an aloe vera plant when you left.

At this point you began to realise that you had no idea what a PhD actually was. All you knew was that your dad had one, in Electronic Engineering, and his had gone so well he went to America and met Bill Gates. Oh, and you had also seen PhD students around campus and knew what they looked like. So you bought yourself a few cardigans, to fit in, and practised your lunch conversation with Bill Gates, just in case.

So here you are now, you clever thing, sitting in your flat with a load of cardigans and an empty computer screen. What are you going to do first? Well, before you can write anything on that lovely clean screen of yours, you're going to have to do some reading.

To the library!

Once there, take out books with the determination of a contestant on Supermarket Sweep. You told your funders you were going to research 'representations of visual impairment in literature', because it sounded impressive, so grab anything you can find about eyes and the lack of eyes and representations of the lack of eyes and How To Do a PhD and anything with a pretty cover.

Blimey, aren't books heavy? You'd never noticed before.

When you lug the books down to the front desk, hot and sweaty in your cardigan, ask the librarian: 'What's the maximum number of books I can take out in one go?' 'I don't know for a PhD,' he will say. 'But it's a lot.'

Smile and look at the queue behind you, hoping everyone heard that. *I don't know for a PhD*, he said. *For a PhD*. That's right, folks: a PhD! Ask for a plastic bag to put the books in and step outside into the rain.

At home, decide you are going to need a special shelf. Box up your self-help books and put your PhD books in their place. Sit at your desk and look at the shelf.

Make a cup of tea.

Watch *The Apprentice* on iPlayer.

Wonder what the term 'original research' means.

Go out to a nightclub with your friends and dance to *The A-Team* theme music.

Three days later, go to the special shelf, take a book, and begin to read. The book is about blind chimpanzees in Central Africa. Decide to write a PhD on 'The correlation between visually-impaired chimpanzees in Central Africa and blind characters in the early novels of Charles Dickens'. Because it sounds impressive.

Open a new Word document and write that down. Then spend two and a half hours googling for correlations between visually-impaired chimpanzees in Central Africa and blind characters in the early novels of Charles Dickens. Huh, well how about that? No luck.

Whew, you have just attended your sixth supervisor meeting, and thank goodness these exist.

Your supervisor has asked you to stop creating Word documents containing impressive-sounding titles, and to spend your time reading instead. 'Your angle will come,' he says mysteriously, and you can't help blushing at his use of the word *come*.

Decide that you are in love with your supervisor. Treat yourself to a new cardigan for your next meeting.

It is now half a year since you started, and your deliciously handsome supervisor has suggested you apply for a scholarship to study at the Library of Congress for a few months. In America. Five hundred and thirty eight miles of books, he says, and you picture the two of you, running naked through the English Literature section, kissing by Milton and boning by Chaucer.

Miraculously, your application for a scholarship is successful, and you fly out to Capitol Hill. There, you live with two guys; one of whom is a furniture salesman, and the other of whom works in Congress. It is the start of summer, and every time you step out of the door you feel like you are being slapped in the face with a hot, wet flannel. Throw away those cardigans, girlfriend!

At the library, there is a special Center ('er'), where you have your own workspace, and there is a filter coffee machine, and you have to get your bags checked every day on the way in and out, and you feel Very Important Indeed.

Go for beers after work with your new academic friends. Get so drunk you lose your way home and fall asleep on the steps of the Capitol building. Get found by the police. When they ask where you live, tell them you can't remember. (It starts with a… no, wait…) Let them take your phone and call your housemate, telling him to come and collect you. As he drives you back home at four in the morning, don't forget to tell him how sorry you are, at least once every five seconds. And cry as hard as you can when he informs you that you were asleep under his office window.

Spend the next day in bed, phoning your ex-boyfriend, your mother, your father, your sister, your friends. Get back with your ex-boyfriend, because a long-distance relationship is just what you need.

What you also need is routine: so find one. Arrive at the library for half nine. Leave at four. Read voraciously. Develop an interest in the representation of blind women in nineteenth-century literature. Come up with a groundbreaking theory about the description of prostitutes' eyes in the novels of Charles Dickens. Email your supervisor. Consider ending it with a kiss.

Spend evenings listening to your housemates debating politics. Understand about one sentence in ten. Go to a peacock farm owned by the furniture salesman's aunt. Lie on a sun-lounger by the pool and wonder whether getting back with your ex-boyfriend was a good idea.

Holy guacamole! You have a full draft of your PhD!

Near the end of the scholarship, your dad comes to visit. Proudly show him your place at the library. Books here, computer there, filter coffee machine over there. Take him to the Brown Bag Lunch and listen to your friend Guido play a tune on the library's Stradivarius. Does your dad look impressed? Of course he does.

Take a couple of days out from the library to go to New Orleans with your dad. *Norlins*, he tells you. You have to pronounce it *Norlins*. Listen to a jazz band on the Mississippi. Take a horse and cart ride around the French quarter. Visit the voodoo museum.

On your dad's last night in America, stay up late discussing your PhD Sparkle as he tells you how proud he is. Listen carefully as he tells you how bored he gets because he has no-one to talk to about clever things. Nod when he tells you he thinks he has Asperger's Syndrome, that he can't connect with the world around him. Ask him if that's why he drinks so much. Get him to promise to see a doctor about his hernia when he gets back. Tell him you love him more than anyone else in the world.

When you get back to Scotland, break up with your ex-boyfriend. Shortly after that get a phone call from your dad. His hernia is sorted, he says, but now he has cancer.

See a psychiatrist.

Fly to Disneyland with a man you have known for just two days. Then Prague with a man you have known two weeks. Consider this progress. Receive feedback from your supervisor. Edit. Edit.

See a psychologist.

Go to England and feel shocked at how ill your dad looks. Think about quitting your PhD. He tells you how proud he is of you for doing it, so don't quit, don't ever quit, just keep on going.

Back in Scotland, double your dose of antidepressants. Stop eating properly. Cry after two glasses of wine. Get herpes. Completely rewrite your entire PhD in a fortnight. (You have ditched the early nineteenth century, and are now looking exclusively at the fin de siècle. The fin de siècle is where it's at, dude.) Get a new boyfriend: Simon. Watch endless episodes of *Come Dine With Me* but stop cooking. Return all your library books and put the self-help books back in their place.

How to Cope with Depression.
Pulling Your Own Strings.
A Rough Guide to Grief.

Phone home several times a day. Your mum tells you she wants a divorce. Your sister tells you she wants to die. Your dad tells you he wants to live.

Try cognitive behavioural therapy. Come off the antidepressants. Ask your supervisor out on a date and cry when he says no. Cry after one glass of wine. Tell your supervisor he is a total prick. (But delete the email before you hit send.)

Rewrite the entire PhD again, this time only using words beginning with the letter 'c'. Come home early from a nightclub and cut yourself with a razor. Tear off a piece of the aloe vera plant and squeeze the gel onto your wound. Go back on the antidepressants. Develop a headache. Go for a brain scan.

Hurray for you, hurray for you.

Make a list of your losses over the last ten years. Map them out on A3 paper and colour-code them. Brain scan tests inconclusive. Go home for Father's Day. Decorate the patio in chalk. Draw hearts and stars and write 'I love you Graham's number' and tie balloons and streamers to the silver birch tree by the back door. Watch your dad walk across the patio with his Zimmer Frame and tears in his eyes.

Just before you leave, your dad whispers something: *go on lots of adventures for me.*

Cry on the train all the way back to Glasgow.

Move in with Simon. Phone your dad and ask his advice on plastering walls. Wish him luck for his hospital appointment tomorrow.

Build a bed.

Find a missed call from your mum the next morning.

Seven hours later, arrive at the train station. Buy a cheese and onion sandwich for your dad and head for the hospital. Wonder why your mum has stopped replying to your texts. Walk through the hospital wondering where all the people are. Find the oncology ward and reach for the door handle. A nurse stops you. 'Haven't you heard?'

In a darkened room, you see your sister and your mum, your aunt and your uncle.

A few moments later, see your first dead body. Touch it. Talk to it. Say goodbye to it.

Drink. Cry. Edit.

It's snowing outside. Put on a cardigan. Fuck it, put on two.

Buy an extra pair of tights because your legs sting so badly in the cold, then walk tentatively towards your viva. A viva is an exam where you get to discuss the research you've done over the last four years. To show the examiners why you are an expert, why you deserve to be a Doctor. It's the most satisfying part of your whole PhD, your dad once told you.

Two hours later, the viva is over.

Try not to slip over in the snow on the way out, and head for the nearest bar. All your friends are waiting for you. They have cards and presents, balloons and streamers. Down two glasses of champagne and open your presents.

What's wrong with a PhD composed entirely with words beginning with the letter 'c', you ask. What's wrong with those *cunting cocks – can't* they *cope* with the *concept*?

Consider writing a letter to Margaret Atwood or Bill Gates. Consider writing a letter to your dad, telling him how relieved you are he's not here to see you fail.

Hurray for you.

Wonder what the hell a PhD is anyway. Then do all that you know how to do. Write.

Butterflies

Like the story of life itself, this tale begins with a small, pale circle.

I was living alone in a tenement flat in the West End of Glasgow. The flat had a spare room, a dining table, a piano, and the Internet. I'd started renting it after breaking up with Leon. Leon had helped me move in – we carried in the furniture, had sex on the carpet, then I bought him a pint and we went our separate ways.

Mum used to love driving up from England to visit me here.

'Sorry I'm late,' she said, arriving at my front door one afternoon. 'Traffic was terrible.' She put down her things and we went into the living room.

'Look at you,' Mum marvelled.

I'd been going to the gym a lot, and was getting toned.

Mum, it transpired, had been exercising too. 'Let's compare bodies,' she suggested, so I closed the curtains and we stripped to our underwear.

Using the tape measure from my sewing kit, we checked our thighs, our waists, our arms, and our breasts. Mum had brought a special machine with her, which calculated how much fat you had. It turned out our bodies were almost identical.

We rubbed fake tan into each other's skin and dressed ourselves.

After that we took a walk in the West End. We went to delis and boutiques, and Mum sighed over skinny lattes, saying how much she'd love to live in a place like this, in a flat like mine, with a life like mine.

That evening, she grabbed her phone and announced that she was going for a walk. An hour later she returned with a bottle of wine. 'Okay if I check my emails?'

She took my laptop, and the wine, into the spare room and closed the door.

In the morning, she called me to her room. 'Look at this.' She was holding out her palm. In it was a small, pale circle.

'What's that?' I asked.

'Contraception,' she said. 'Stops the sperm getting to the egg. Touch it.'

'Um. No thanks.' I went to make breakfast.

When Mum left that afternoon, I looked at my Internet history. Sites visited: *Gmail* (once); *thetrainline* (twice); and something called *Butterflies In My Tummy* (multiple times).

I typed *butterfliesinmytummy.com* into the search bar, and was automatically redirected to a new site: *www.lawlessencounters.co.uk*.

'Married but Feeling neglected?' it said, capital 'F' for feeling. 'In need of an exiting encounter?' (Yes, exiting.) 'Try our extra-marital dating service. You'll get butterflies in your tummy.'

After a quick search, I could see that there were over 300 people registered on the site who lived in Buckinghamshire alone. The same phrases appeared again and again.

Discretion is a must.
Mornings are best for me.
Since we had the kids, the spark has gone.
I like socialising.
I am slightly eccentric.
I have no intention of leaving my partner.

And their pictures; half of them with heads missing, just torsos and limbs.

I could see that my mum had been chatting to a guy called KristianB. I searched for his profile. Swansea, two kids. 'My marriage is perfect in every way except that the physical side has fizzled out. I enjoy weightlifting and wine.'

Sitting at the dining table, I picked up my phone. Three missed calls before I got through.

'I've pulled in at a service station. What is it, love?'

'I checked my computer,' I said. 'I know what you were doing.'

'What do you mean?'

'I've seen that website.'

She hung up.

Half an hour later, she phoned back. 'I can't believe you've been spying on me!' she shouted. 'Anyway, it's my life, and I haven't done anything wrong. It's not like I'm meeting anyone. Just chatting. I get lonely. I haven't done anything wrong.'

She hung up again.

A birthday tea was being prepared: sandwiches, crisps, jelly and ice-cream. My sister was turning twenty-five. Her mental health was deteriorating rapidly. She had quit her job at the library, and, after one suicide attempt too many, had been taken into psychiatric hospital. The hospital had agreed to let her come home for her birthday, so Grandma and Granddad had driven down from Stalybridge, and everyone was going out of their way to make it the perfect day.

Before tea, Dad asked if I fancied a walk.

'Shall we *all* go?' Mum asked brightly.

'I quite fancy just going with my Greta,' Dad said, and I glowed with love.

As we left the driveway and walked along the roadside, Dad stayed quiet. After just minutes of strolling, he was out of breath.

'I've almost finished my PhD,' I told him.

'Yeah?'

'I'd love it if you could read it.'

He stopped for a moment to rest. 'My PSA levels are getting worse.'

I stopped too. 'I thought they were stable.'

'I'm afraid they're rising again. The doctors have told me–'

'Told you what?'

'That if I don't start chemo, I've got about ten weeks left.'

He started walking again.

I used every ounce of energy I had to follow him. *I'll allow myself the biggest crying fit I've ever had later on*, I thought. *As soon as I'm on my own, I'll cry until my insides fall out.*

A little further up the road, we stopped again. 'Let's rest here.' Dad took a cigar out of his jacket pocket and I sat on the fence beside him.

I looked out over the fields, at the leaves beginning to reappear on the trees.

'Can you keep a secret?' Dad asked suddenly.

My heart fluttered.

'I'm not talking about a little secret,' he said. 'I'm talking about something big. So big that you can never tell anyone about it. Not even Simon.' Simon was my new boyfriend. 'And not your Grandma or Granddad, your sister, or anyone.'

'Er, I don't know, Dad.'

'Promise me.'

I looked down at my legs as they hit against the fence. One... two... three... 'Okay. I promise.'

'It's your mum,' he said. 'I'm afraid she's mentally ill.'

'What?'

'She thinks she's deleted her emails, but I understand things about computers she never will.'

'What do you mean?'

'She had an affair.'

I instantly remembered KristianB, the guy with the 'perfect marriage', who liked weightlifting and wine.

'That's over now,' Dad continued, 'but since she broke up with him she's been having sex with other people. Lots of other people. Hundreds of other people,' he told me. 'Smoking crack and going to sex parties. Dungeons! Dungeons in Milton Keynes, Greta. Can you imagine it? I'm worried she's going to get in trouble with the police.' He took several long drags on his cigar. 'I want you to promise to look after her when I die.'

I looked at my hands for a moment, wondered how they had always managed to stay so small, had barely grown since I was a little girl. Then I slid off the fence and held my dad tight. I felt his thinning hair, and his scalp smeared with a thick layer of sweat. I knew that there was once a time, a long stretch of time, when Dad was the one cheating on my mum. When he two and even three-timed her, when he abandoned her before their wedding day, when he had affairs while my sister and I were babies. I also knew that my mum had remained completely faithful to him throughout it all.

I heard him take another drag of his cigar behind my back.

'Don't worry about me,' he said when I pulled away. 'I've started taking antidepressants. They're magic.'

I felt a stabbing pain in my gut.

'Do you promise?' he asked.

'Promise what?'

'That you'll look after her.'

'I don't know. Yes. I'll try.'

'Okay. We've got to go back now.'

I'd almost forgotten: my sister's birthday tea.

'When we get back,' he told me, 'you're not going to say a word about this. You're going to go in there and you're going to give your mum the biggest hug in the world.' He looked into my eyes. 'I know you're a good actress, Greta,' he said. 'You're about to do the best performance of your life.'

The howl that I gave in the garden that evening was a howl that shook my bones; that shook the earth beneath my feet; and that shook the whole world I had known up to that very point in my existence.

'Your mum's got a designer vagina,' Dad announced, late one night over the phone.

I was shaking, but couldn't seem to hang up.

'She's had her labia chopped off.'

'Please, Dad, I–'

'She's a slut, your mum. A *slut*.'

'Dad, are you on your own? What are you doing?'

He was quiet for a moment, then I heard him exhale: a cigar. All his pauses were filled with smoke these days. 'I'm at home. Graham's here.' Graham worked for my dad, and the call of duty often extended outside of office hours.

'Okay. That's good. You're not still drinking, are you?' I wasn't sure Dad should be drinking *anything* during the chemo, let alone getting into this state.

'No, no. We've stopped now. Graham's made me a cup of tea.'

'Good. How long is he staying?'

'I don't know. I've thrown your mum's dildos onto the front lawn.'

I pictured an army of thick, veiny rods of purple and pink, raining down onto the grass from the bedroom window, shuddering and squirming as they hit the ground, then sputtering out, still and glistening, like chrysalises in the moonlight.

'There's a lot you don't know about your mum,' Dad growled.

And there's a lot I *do*, I thought.

'What-t-t-t?' my sister finally answered her phone, after several missed calls. 'I can't really talk right now, Gretchen.'

'I'm just missing you,' I said, trying not to let her hear

my tears. 'Wanted to see how you are. Fancied a chat. How's hospital? Spoken to Mum or Dad recently?'

'This isn't a good time.'

'What are you doing?'

'I've run away,' she said. Her teeth were chattering.

'Where are you?'

She hung up.

I sat on the small IKEA table by the window and looked out onto the street. I was living in a horrible flat now. No dining table, no piano, no spare room, no Internet. It was the only way I could afford to keep buying train tickets home to see Dad. My eyes re-focused from the darkness outside to the shape of my reflection in the glass. I was a mess.

I tried calling my sister again. No reply. And again. No reply. Then: 'I don't know where I am, Gretchen. I've been walking for hours. My phone's about to run out of battery.'

'Well… are you near any landmarks? What can you see?'

'Why should I tell you?'

'Please, just tell me what you can see.'

'I can't see anything. It's dark. It's snowing. I'm cold.'

'Find a road sign. Are you near a road?'

'I'm going to sit in the ditch until I die.'

She hung up.

I phoned my mum. 'Oh for god's sake. I'm trying to have a nice dinner with Fern. Why does she always do this to me?'

'What should I do, Mum?'

'I don't know, Gretchen. I'm at my wit's end. I'm exhausted. I've run out of ideas.'

Another hang-up.

Minutes later, my sister called back. 'It says Aldbury,'

she said. 'I found a sign. My phone's about to run out. I'm going to sit in a ditch now.'

I phoned the psychiatric hospital, who hadn't even noticed she was missing, so I called the police. 'I'm afraid there's nothing we can do,' they told me. 'Sounds like she's crossed the border into the next county. Not our area. You'll have to phone the Hertfordshire police.' So I did.

Dad texted me in the middle of the night.

02.20
Have you heard from Mum?

02.20
No.

02.21
Probably out shagging.

02.22
Maybe she's at Fern's. Try and get some sleep.

03.20
I've chucked her butt plugs out the back door.

03.21
**Dad, I'm worried
about you.**

03.30
Are you okay?

03.42
Dad? xxx

04.21
**Did you know
Leon is another
of your Mum's
conquests?**

I called him straight away. 'What are you talking about?'

'Your mum slept with Leon while you were doing your PhD scholarship in America. She slept with your boyfriend.'

'No she didn't.'

'I've read her emails, Gretchen.'

'What did they say?'

'That time she came up to your flat while you were in America. She took him for a curry.'

'No.'

'I'm sorry to have to tell you, love.'

'She didn't.'

'She's not well.'

'Dad.'

'She's mentally ill. A nymphomaniac. A lesbian. A whore.'

'No, Dad.'

'And that time she came to your flat and she was late. Shagged some guy in a motel on the way up.'

'Dad, I can't talk about this. Please get some sleep. I have to switch my phone off now.'

I hung up, then jumped onto my bed and stood on the mattress. *She didn't, she didn't, she didn't,* I muttered, over and over again, until finally I collapsed.

'Dad's chemo has gone so well he might live for another two years,' Mum told me.

The doctor had signed me off my studies for six weeks. I'd discussed Dad's accusation with Mum, who said it was a lie, and I even Skyped Leon, who was teaching English in Thailand, and he said it was a lie too. Mum told me not to believe everything Dad said. He's desperate, she told me. He's paranoid. The cancer has spread to his brain.

At the doctor's advice, I imposed a curfew on my parents: I switched off my phone between the hours of 9 p.m. and 9 a.m. I'd been prescribed diazepam: one tablet per phone call, or two per day during visits home.

'Obviously I don't want him to die,' Mum said, 'but I don't know if I can cope with this for another two years.'

I told her that that I didn't know if I could either.

'He's told everyone at the pub I've been having affairs.'

'Oh dear.'

'And he's ordered a load of Viagra off the Internet,' she added. 'Says if I don't have sex with him he'll file for a divorce.'

I reached for my diazepam.

'I think your dad's going to kill me,' Mum confided in

me one evening. 'We're going on holiday to Zakynthos, to a remote place full of winding roads, and I think he's going to drive us both off a cliff. Here's what I want you to do if I die.'

But Dad didn't kill her. While they were on holiday, Dad's younger brother – my uncle – died after a long battle with Parkinson's, and he spent most of the holiday on the phone to me, crying. When they got back, Mum moved into the spare room at Dad's request. But without Mum there, Dad found it harder than ever to sleep. Sometimes, Mum told me, he would take a pillow into the porch, and stay on the phone to the Samaritans until the early hours. Other times, when he came back from the pub and was too drunk to find his house key, he'd lie on the patio under the stars, shivering on the slabs until he fell asleep.

'They're going to let me try chemo one last time,' Dad told me, after an unexpectedly fast drop in his PSA levels.

Mum had moved back into the main bedroom, but Dad couldn't get upstairs any more. He was sleeping in his office; the local hospital had lent us a bed. It seemed fitting, somehow, that Dad now lived in a room surrounded by computers: the machines he could always rely on.

For the last few months, Dad had been referring to his secretary, Louise, as his 'girlfriend'. He'd taken her and her five-year-old son on holiday to Lapland two weeks before Christmas. My sister and I had been on that very same trip with him when we were that age. But recently, the 'relationship' with Louise had been reduced to a series of text messages. Dad was working from home most of the time now, as he wasn't well enough to drive to work.

Sometimes he wasn't well enough to do any work at all.

Mum, on the other hand, swore she had stopped having affairs. Actually it seemed plausible, since most of her time was taken up looking after Dad and my sister. My sister was out of hospital more than she was in it these days, though she still needed constant attention, and Dad had to wear nappies and surgical stockings, because his legs and feet were so full of fluid. His face had swollen up too, with the steroids, and he was using a Zimmer frame to walk even the most meagre of distances.

'It'll be a different chemical for the chemo this time,' Dad said. 'I've read the list of side effects. It could make the whites of my eyes turn blue. How cool is that?'

'You should come back for a visit soon, love.' I'd imagined this conversation so many times before that hearing it now was a déjà vu. 'The hospital appointment is not going well.'

I sat on my bed and grabbed a fistful of duvet. 'Should I come today? What sort of ticket should I get? An open return? Shall I meet you at the hospital?'

'Your dad's still barely sleeping,' she told me. 'And when he does, it's not on the bed any more. It's too painful for him.' She paused. 'Last week, I got up in the middle of the night to check he was okay. I found him in his armchair, head thrown back, with all the lights on, and the windows open.' Her voice cracked. 'There were moths flying around his head.'

My knuckles, still holding the duvet, had turned white. 'Mum? Are you okay?'

'I'm okay,' she said, with a forced laugh. 'I've bought some new outfits and I'm going to show my face at the pub again soon, put on some make-up, let everyone see I'm doing fine.'

I remained silent.

I could hear Mum breathing, the way she kept swallowing away gulps of air, and I knew she wanted to say something. Eventually, she whispered: 'I still love him, you know.' And then she began to cry.

With those words, I knew that Dad was about to die. And that Mum had just become a butterfly.

The Easiest Thing I Know

Seeing two people at the same time is child's play. All you need is: a piece of string, an egg box, some strong adhesive, and a microwaveable meal for one.

Here's how it's done.

When Alpha asks where you fancy going for dinner, suggest Stravaigan. It's four days since you last saw one another, and that was only for a cup of tea. Now it's Friday night, so it's important to pick somewhere half-decent.

Arrive at the restaurant twenty minutes late, and let Alpha give you a peck on the cheek. As you sit down, quickly check your phone for messages from Omega, then say: 'This looks nice.'

'Doesn't it?' says Alpha, trying to act casual, trying to act like he didn't arrive here twenty minutes early and hasn't already studied the menu a hundred times.

Order a white wine spritzer, and he'll order a second pint, then stroke each other's hands as you wait for your haggis / fisherman's pie to appear. You've been together for nearly eight months. You're finally able to stop talking about your dead father, and rely mainly on how's-your-day-been chat instead. So:

He asks you about your job. You laugh off the comment your boss made about your skirt today. You ask him about his music. He tells you he's started a new track. You cheers to that. The food arrives.

Your meals give you something to discuss for at least five minutes. The haggis is splendid, you both agree, but the fisherman's pie is a little dry. After that, conversation wanders to what such-and-such said about such-a-thing, and what so-and-so should have done but never did, and then it meanders into observations on the other diners in the room, and how silly they all are compared to you.

After dinner, you have another two drinks each, and then you suggest going back to your place.

While you sit on the sofa, rubbing your stomach, trying not to fart, he tells you that the track he made today is in three different time signatures. Excuse yourself, go to the loo, and release as much trapped wind as possible.

Clean your teeth and put on your pyjamas. Climb into bed with a sigh. Remember to set your alarm for the morning, in case you never stop dreaming.

Switch off the light and wait for Alpha to touch your face. This is your cue. Remove your pyjama bottoms while he takes off his boxers, then climb on top of him and indulge in a quick sixty-nine. Sit on his erection before it disappears, and grind your hips until he comes.

Go to the toilet for a wee and a wash, plus a quick pfft pfft pfft because the haggis is still repeating on you, then get back into bed and fall asleep like spoons.

In the morning, before the alarm goes off, creep into the kitchen and take an egg box out of the fridge. Do the following:

1. Place the eggs in a bowl.
2. Put the bowl in the fridge.
3. Take the empty egg box into the living room.
4. Find a piece of string, then cut it into small strands.
5. Glue the strands to the top of the egg box using a strong adhesive.
6. Draw two circles on the top half of the box.
7. Take your creation into the bedroom.

Alpha looks beautiful when he is sleeping. His hair is so soft you can't help but run your fingers through it.

Sit on the edge of the bed and hold up the egg box. Open it, then close it, and repeat this movement, making the egg box talk. 'Good morning,' it whispers. 'What shall we do today?'

Alpha rubs his eyes. 'What time is it?'

'It's almost ten,' says the egg box.

'Yikes, I need to go and finish that track,' he says.

'Really? Now?'

'Aprovecha el momento, my dear,' he replies. 'Aprovecha el momento.'

'What are you talking about?'

'Take advantage of the moment.'

'Isn't it bad to take advantage?'

The alarm goes off.

The egg box sits safely in your handbag when you leave the flat around midday.

You are in a new dress and new boots, and a pair of black lacy knickers, which, despite one small tear above the left thigh, are your favourite pair. Your hair is straight and you've got an umbrella, so even if it rains it's staying that way.

After a wander around the Botanics, and a few errands (posting a letter, phoning your mum, buying some tampons), you head to Kelvinbridge. When you're three blocks away, give Omega a call. This gives him time to clean his teeth and put on his shoes.

Now wait outside the subway station, dipping the toes of your boots into puddles and watching the rainwater creep up the leather. Wonder why the soundtrack from the film *Evita* is stuck in your head.

Omega appears in a hoodie and jeans. 'You look gorgeous,' he says, grabbing your bum and pulling you close. His tongue, still coated in toothpaste, delves between your lips.

After looking quickly left and right to check no-one is watching, drag Omega into the subway station. Ride the subway to St. Enoch, and from there, walk down to the river. The rain has stopped but it's breezy. Pull a hair out of your mouth before you speak. Then, with urgency, say: 'I'd very much like to go to Buenos Aires.'

'Why?' Omega will ask.

Lean over the railing and look down onto the river. 'Because I've heard it's like Paris,' you tell him. 'Only further away.'

Omega leans over the railing beside you.

Look into his eyes, wondering whether to kiss him again, but instead, reach into your handbag and pull out the egg box. 'Well,' you make the box say. 'What are we going to do now?'

Omega looks at the egg box, then at you. 'Fancy a drink?'

Hold onto him with your left hand, keeping the egg box firmly in your right, and walk along the river until you spy an off-licence on a nearby road. Omega returns with a six pack of lager, and you sit on a bench by the river and drink, covering the labels with your fingers so that the cans could be mistaken for coke.

'This is nice,' says the egg box, halfway through your second can. 'It's not Argentina, but it's nice.' The tips of your fingers are turning blue.

Omega sticks his hand down his trousers to rearrange himself. 'God I want you,' he says. 'Shall we go back to mine?'

'I was thinking,' you purr, 'we could do something romantic. Aprovecha el momento.'

'Romantic? Like what?'

'A midnight picnic.'

'It's two in the afternoon.'

'A picnic, then.'

Omega goes back to the off-license, and comes back with cheese and onion crisps, pork scratchings, and a packet of beef jerky.

'It'll have to do,' sighs the egg box.

You walk along the river a bit more, sliding your feet over the sludgy ground until you reach some bushes. Lay out the picnic, then sit on a carrier bag and open the beef jerky.

Omega unbuttons your duffel coat. He puts his hand down your tights. 'Oh yeah,' he says.

Chew on a piece of beef jerky as he fingers you.

As you drink your last can of beer, the egg box talks about Buenos Aires. 'The whole place is full of silver,' it says. 'And everyone is madly in love.'

Omega wipes his hand on his trousers, and asks if you're ready to go back to his.

'I don't know,' you say. 'Maybe you should ask the egg box.'

Omega says, 'I'd like to fuck you in the arse.'

On the way back from Omega's house, you rub your stomach, which is no longer full of wind, but now aches from leaning over the sofa on two separate occasions; the first while Omega pumped you for the entire length of a James Bond movie, and the second while he jerked off over you to *Mock the Week*. Put a thumb to your hairline and feel the hair, clumped and brittle.

Stop off at the supermarket and buy yourself a steak. Argentina is famous for its red meat.

As soon as you step through your front door, take off all your clothes. Wash yourself, first with aqueous cream, then with shower gel. Put on your pyjamas and call Alpha.

'I'm lonely,' you tell him.

'I'm getting on really well with this track,' he replies. 'Have you read the article on Borderline Personality Disorder I sent you yet?'

Lie on your bed and text Omega, who texts back immediately to say that next time he sees you he's going to make spunk fly out of your eyeballs. Kiss kiss.

Go online and read the Lonely Planet Guide to Buenos Aires.

Wander into the kitchen and put the steak on the counter. You could only afford frying steak, and it's very thin and wrinkled. Looks like a vulva. Hide it with a tea towel and scour the fridge for something else.

Spot the bowl of eggs on the top shelf.

Crack two eggs into a pan and make yourself an omelette.

As you eat, begin to cry.

Put on the film *Last Tango in Paris* and cry some more.

When you finish the eggs, reflect on your choice of meal. Convince yourself that if you had bought a microwaveable meal for one, you would not feel this way just now.

Take the egg box out of your handbag. Stare into its big biro eyes. 'I'm sorry,' you say, and then stamp on it.

Later that night, while you are in bed, a child wails in the flat beneath yours. Lie still, and don't breathe again until you hear the trudge of parent's feet and the creak of a door, then the gentle lullaby the mother sings. It's a different lullaby to the one your mother used to sing to you. The one she sang you went:

Backe, backe Kuchen!
Der Bäcker hat gerufen.
Wer will guten Kuchen backen,
Der muss haben sieben Sachen:
Eier und Schmalz,
Zucker und Salz,
Milch und Mehl,
Safran macht den Kuchen gelb.
Schieb, shieb in den Ofen 'rein!
(Morgen muss er fertig sein.)

It means something like this:

Bake, bake cakes!
The baker has called.
He who wants to bake good cakes
Must have seven things:
Eggs and lard,
Sugar and salt,
Milk and flour,
Saffron makes the cake yellow.
Shove, shove it in the oven!
(Tomorrow it must be done.)

Decide to call your mother in the morning. Don't forget to set your alarm – in case you don't stop dreaming – then sleep, go to sleep, like a baby.

A Rough Guide To Grief

Everyone grieves differently. There is no right or wrong way to do it. Your grief is personal to you. It is unique.

However.

Unique is a very strong word, isn't it?

Actually, many people who grieve report remarkably similar experiences, and it can be really helpful to share such things.

What you'll find here are a few hints and tips on how to cope with your grief. A *rough guide* to grief, as it were. You may want to keep it somewhere handy over the coming weeks and months: on a bedside table, by the phone, or next to the kitchen knives, for instance, and refer to it when you are feeling bad.

You may also find it helpful to talk through the guide with your doctor, family and friends, or you may want to look at it in private, seething at its poor use of apostrophes and over-reliance on the passive voice. If the latter, try drawing moustaches on the people in the photographs to let off steam. Whatever works for you.

At First

Initially, you may find you are in shock. Even though you cried when you saw the dead body, lying there so cold and yellow, with its downturned mouth and shattered eyes, you may find it hard to believe that any of this has really happened.

You may surprise yourself by how strong you are as you walk away from the hospital, having kissed the corpse goodbye. As you cross the car park trying to remember where you left the bloody car, you may even find yourself joking about the fact that without your loved one here to guide you, you could end up roaming this patch of concrete for all eternity, a ghost just like him.

When you try to eat that night, you may be astonished to discover how great your appetite is, and you may even try a glass of red wine, just a small one, and do a cheers in your loved one's honour, followed by an anecdote about the time he tried to warm up Frisky the lamb in the Aga when it was ill, and – oh, ho, the tears of laughter will stream down your face – how that poor little lamb jumped out of the scalding oven! You won't know where this anecdote came from. You haven't told that one for years. Everyone will laugh.

If you find you are not able to cry in the days following the death, make the most of this stoic strength, and spend your time:

- making funeral arrangements,
- cancelling credit cards,
- changing your loved one's Facebook status to 'dead',
- visiting the solicitor,
- watching *The Antiques Roadshow*,
- learning the implication of words like Estate and Beneficiary and Bequest,
- using the 'F word' in public,

- cleaning out the wardrobe of all your loved one's clothes, and setting fire to them at the bottom of the garden,
- except for that one red shirt, you know the one, it still smells of him: that one you must keep forever.

It is worth noting at this point how difficult the funeral will be. But if you choose not to have one – well, good luck to you.

Once the shock of the person dying begins to subside, and this can take a very long time, you may find your emotions become stronger. You may feel 'up' one minute, and 'down' the next, as if you are on an emotional rollercoaster. You may start using a lot more metaphors and similes than you used to do. *I have a knot in the pit of my stomach. I'm drowning. It's as if someone has just ripped out my heart and is standing there in front of me, holding it up to my face, while the blood drips all over my feet.* Such phrases are not uncommon.

It is likely you will get ill shortly after your loved one has died. You tried to remain strong for so long, but now that your loved one is dead your immune system is at an all-time low. Though it may feel like something more serious, it will probably just be a cold or a prolonged bout of insomnia. It is not unheard of for the recently bereaved to shit themselves or get terrible acne or a verruca or two. If this happens, don't panic, just use the creams as your doctor advises.

Some of you may start to hallucinate. It may be the smell of his cigar smoke, or his hand brushing your cheek, or you may even see him sitting at the kitchen table, pulling faces behind your mother's back, trying to lighten the mood. Remember: people pay good money for visions such as this. So enjoy the trip.

Later

Grief takes time. That's worth repeating. Grief takes time.

In fact, you'll be amazed by how much of your time is taken by grief.

And just when you think you're almost done grieving, you'll find something sets you off again. The smell of Heinz tomato soup. 'Starman' by David Bowie. Paper clips. The new series of *Doctor Who*. In such scenarios, don't despair. Your grief will come and go. You need to grieve, just as you need to live.

Do things that make you feel better. Go for a walk. See friends for tea. Make a scrapbook. Become completely obsessed with sex because it feels like 'the opposite of death'. Apply for bereavement counselling. Get very, very drunk and call the Samaritans and tell them you want to die. See friends for cake. Cut a cross into each of your thighs with a razor blade. Go swimming once the wounds are healed.

You may find you need to talk about the person who has died over and over again. In truth, you may become a bit of a bore. At this point you will begin to discover who your real friends are. The real friends will come out to meet you when it's minus four degrees outside, your eyes are bloodshot and hair a mess, and all you want to do is drink beer and talk about how much you wish your loved one had left you a message or a token of some sort to keep and remember him by.

Unfortunately, some of the people you thought were your friends will turn out to be your enemies. They will not forgive you when you forget to make a phone call, or when you get irritable over nothing, or when you have to cancel on them because you have just shit your pants but are too scared to admit it. Instead, they will write you nasty emails and call you rude names and block you on Twitter. Well let me tell you now: you don't need people like that. They can fuck right off.

Besides, if you want, you can make new friends. Make friends with people who have grieved. Make friends with people who are grieving. Make friends with people who are dying. Make friends with death. You will be very close in the end.

Eventually

Here's a phrase you'll hear a lot while you're grieving: it gets better.

Some of your 'friends who have grieved' will delight in telling you this as often as possible. The good news for you is that you will soon have earned the right to tell this to other people, those who are just starting out on their journey. It gets better, you will say, and you will pat them on the shoulder, and then go back to your flat and cut a swearword into your shin, which is a shame, because you thought you were over that, but never mind: it gets better.

Certain events are always going to be tricky. Birthdays, Christmas, Father's Day, the Anniversary Of His Death. This last one is a brand new date to add to your diary for the rest of time. On difficult days such as these, you may find it helps to be around family. You could even perform a ceremony to remember your loved one, perhaps lighting a candle or sending a Chinese lantern up into the sky, but try not to set fire to yourself, as this will make you feel worse.

Waking up will eventually become less painful, as will going to sleep. In due course, you may even find that you don't need to drink two bottles of wine or take three diazepams or have unprotected sex with a complete stranger to get you through such things. The world may start to feel a little more real again, and you may start to feel a little more like you.

One day you will realise that you haven't used a simile or a metaphor in over a week, and you will discover that you feel able to cope again. It is around this time that you will get a letter through from the bereavement counsellors saying you are finally at the top of the waiting list, and they are ready to schedule your initial consultation.

Go. I urge you. Even if you think you are done grieving. Even if the thought that you have been on that damn waiting list for the past eight months has you spitting feathers. Even if that is another metaphor, which makes you feel you are regressing. Go to that appointment.

When the old lady with the shawl asks you three A4 pages of difficult personal questions, be honest with her. How close were you to the person that died? Very. Have you finished grieving? No. Have you caused yourself any physical harm since the bereavement? Yes.

At the end of the consultation, with a face full of tears, ask to go to the toilet. The old lady will give you a key, which you must return to her in the busy reception area afterwards. 'I forgot to say,' she'll declare loudly as she takes the key, 'I hope you weren't cutting yourself in there.' Your cheeks will go red. 'Try to stop doing that, missy!' she'll call, waggling her finger as you dash towards the exit.

When you get home, put the letter from the bereavement counsellors in the bin. Call the Samaritans. Watch *The Antiques Roadshow*. Call the Samaritans.

As you lie in bed that night, unable to sleep, try as hard as you can to bring that nagging thought to the front of your mind. What is it? Almost got it. Ah yes, there it is: it happens to us all, sooner or later. And one day, if you ever allow anyone to love you enough, someone will grieve for you too. That's right. Even you.

If You Drank Coffee

And so, since you're my imaginary lover: this is how it would go.

We would be in bed. It would be ten, maybe eleven o'clock. The sun would be shining through the blinds. I would be curved against your body, which would smell of coconut and sleep.

I'd be a little groggy, because – knowing me – I'd have had one or two drinks too many the night before. But even though I'd be tired, due to the booze, I'd also be restless, due to the Prozac. I'd be blinking quicker than usual, sniffing and scratching to use up energy, and I'd be desperately trying not to scream *wake up wake up wake up* in your left ear.

But I wouldn't make a sound. I'd swallow the words and count my own breaths instead.

Eventually I'd be compelled to touch you. I'd run my fingers down the length of your spine; exploring the skin I was lucky enough to be sharing a mattress with. The more that I touched, of course, the more that I'd want to touch – and the more you'd plunge your face between the pillows, trying to disconnect the sensation of my probing hands from the splendour of your sleep.

It would take me a while, but in the end, I'd realise I'm simply an annoyance. I'd stop stroking – and wait.

Nothing would happen for a very long time.

In my head, I'd be walking along the edge of the River Kelvin, or jetting off for a long weekend in Paris, or scribbling hearts on the pavement in chalk, or counting the cracks in the cornicing above my head, and all the while you'd be there, tucked into me, both of us going nowhere, both of us dreaming.

It might be half an hour before you finally awoke. I like to imagine your first words that day would be, 'Hello, my love.' But perhaps they'd be, 'You look wonderful.' Or, 'Ugh. I hate mornings.'

Naturally, I would kiss you – first on the temple, and then on the lips – and I would ask politely how you slept. You'd say 'fine' and ask how I slept, and I'd say 'fine', and, judging by our tossing and turning throughout the night, we would both be telling lies.

After that, I would grasp your arm a little harder than usual, a little more urgently than I had expected, and I would tell you that what I would really, really like to do – right now – would be to stay in bed and *listen* to something. Some music, or a radio play, or the sound of each other's voices, though I daren't say the last one in case you got weird.

At this point you would nod, and say a radio play would be nice.

And I would almost explode with excitement!

I would do anything for you at this moment. If you drank coffee, I would make you a coffee. If you liked toast, I would make you toast. If you wanted the world's biggest hug, I'd give you one of those in an instant. But since you're probably not thirsty, nor hungry, nor looking very touchy-feely right now, as ever, I'd settle for a smile.

I'd switch on the radio and slip back into bed, and for a

second I'd feel disappointed that you didn't put your arm around me. I'd arch my back and bite my lip and you'd see me doing so and ask what's wrong. I would say 'nothing, don't be silly, nothing', and yet you'd wonder – for the whole time I was getting back out of bed and getting the radio to *Come on you bastard, work!* – you'd wonder if there was something else The Matter. But then there'd be the crackle, grunt and groan of serious voices and we'd know that the play was about to start.

We'd stop talking. Sit up straight; pull the covers tight around ourselves. Duvet around you. Duvet around me. Duvet around *us* but with no skin touching.

I like to think that the play would be about a couple. A couple who'd been experiencing a few problems in their relationship, but who'd ultimately be inextricably, unimaginably, *dangerously* romantically entwined. I'd inch my legs towards yours, gasping at the sad bits, smirking at the rude bits, looking at you out of the corner of my eye every five seconds to check that you were still there.

At the end of the play, something would of course happen that would prevent the couple from being together, and I'd probably cry. Who am I kidding? I'd definitely cry. But I already know that you wouldn't shed a tear. Strangely, though, while chatting about it in the bath afterwards, I'd give it a seven out of ten, and you'd wager an eight. Because that's the way we are.

Next, I'd spend about an hour getting ready. It's not ideal, when all *you* have to do is chuck on a t-shirt and trousers and you're the most handsome man in the universe. I, on the other hand, have eyebrows to pluck, hair to straighten, a flabby stomach to disguise, and arms to either hide or highlight, depending on my mood and my menstrual cycle.

Since I'm currently using suppositories to treat my haemorrhoids, I'd also have to take one of those out of the fridge (yes, fridge) and push it into myself. 'Have you taken your bum medicine?' you'd say, and we'd laugh, and it'd be horrible and intimate and wrong, but I'd be glad we could talk about such things or else we'd go mad.

While in the bathroom, I'd also tweezer out that black hair I keep getting in my left nipple, I'd check my verruca wasn't showing signs of reappearing, and I'd think about how many days it was before I was due to start bleeding again. But you wouldn't care whether or not I was doing any of these things. You'd be on the sofa, fiddling with your iPhone, with a faint feeling of contentment running through your bones.

When I was finally ready, we'd leave the flat together – hand in hand – and we'd talk about where to go next. You'd propose going to a café in the West End, and I'd suggest a walk along the edge of the River Kelvin, or jetting off for a long weekend in Paris (joke), or scribbling hearts on the pavement in chalk (joke joke joke joke joke – but not really a joke – but yes, joke), and, inevitably, we'd end up going to a café in the West End. There, we'd sit and count the cracks in the cornicing while we talked.

We'd talk about the past, and we'd talk about the present, and it's highly unlikely that we'd talk about the future, but I'd keep my fingers crossed anyway, just in case today might be the day. We'd eat muffins and eggs, and you wouldn't have coffee, of course, but you'd have orange juice and tea, and occasionally our eyes would meet and stick in the middle of a sentence… and then we'd carry on like it was just a blip.

You'd tell me how well your work was going, and I'd tell you I was getting sexually-harassed by my boss but was too scared to report it, and you'd say that was stupid of me, and I'd get upset, but then you'd say you wanted to chuck a brick through my boss' window, and I'd forgive you.

Perhaps, when you weren't looking, I'd pull down my top a little further than usual, hoping a bit of cleavage might stimulate something fiery deep inside you. I'd lick my lips and think dirty thoughts. But I guess we'd have had sex five or six days ago, which would still be fairly recent for you, so I wouldn't want to push my luck.

After the café, there'd be a trip to buy a puncture repair kit for your bike, and a moment where I'd think I'd lost my wallet but I'd find it two minutes later, and there'd be a discussion about how long it'd be before we would see each other again, and how short it seemed until it got dark these days. And then we'd bid each other farewell.

Me back to my flat; you back to yours.

Simple as that.

And this is about the most perfect day I could ever imagine.

Let's Buy A Keyring So We
Remember This Forever

Her naked body reminded me of my father's corpse.

Yellowing mouth.

Bruises along the arms.

Pinpricks.

Scabs.

You want some, baby?

I lifted a hand to the glass, wondering if she'd raise her palm level with mine.

Her pupils flicked towards me. She wrenched out her chest. Black hair sprung from her scalp in greasy ropes. Medusa.

You want some, baby?

She might have said that. She might have said anything. Or nothing. How could I tell? A pane of glass cut between us.

'Gretchen! You coming?'

Simon's voice. Simon was here. Where were we?

'Gretchen, it's rude to stare. Come on.'

Goodbye, my lips shuddered.

Every window was different. The girls were fat, thin, brown, white, ugly – and some, some were beautiful.

They sat, sprawled, and squirmed. Beckoned, smiled, and pouted. But none of them were quite like my Medusa girl.

'I thought we could check out the Condomerie,' said Simon. 'Be a bit of a giggle. Apparently they do over three-hundred types of–'

'Okay,' I shrugged. 'Let's do it.'

Simon ran his fingers over the map. 'Let's see… We're here… And we need to be there…'

I pointed to a cobbled street ahead. 'It's *that* way.' The thought of having to listen to Simon make a hash of Amsterdam's intricate streets one more time was giving me sinus ache.

'Oh. Right.' He folded up the map, neatly and precisely into exact sixths, and put it safely in the pocket of his 50-tog all-terrain anorak. His fingers reached for mine.

I was shocked at how clammy my hands were. 'I need some gloves.'

'Don't think they sell that sort of *glove* where we're going.' Simon choked out a laugh, so I choked one back.

As we headed down the cobbled street, we passed a shop window full of cuddly toys. Hundreds of neon-pink teddy bears, each with a big, furry erection. A sign above them read: TEDDY BEAR'S DICKNIC.

Simon stopped and took a picture on his iPhone. 'Classic.'

I hurried ahead and feigned surprise. 'Oh look, here it is.'

The shop hadn't changed. In the window was the same row of condoms, pegged on a line like dirty socks.

A woman in a baseball cap shuffled out of the door. 'That was swell,' she called behind her, 'now let's go get somethin' t'eat.'

A man in a baseball cap trailed after her, with a bulging carrier bag. 'I thought you wanted to go back to that Souvenir Shop first, honey?' he puffed. 'Get that keyring you liked?'

I didn't hear the woman's answer, but I hoped that she did go back for that keyring. How else would she remember Amsterdam? Those condoms would get used up, if she was lucky, and all that nice holiday food wasn't coming back – well, not in a way you'd want to keep on your mantelpiece. A keyring on the other hand – a keyring lasts. Every time you open the door to your same-old home back in your same-old town, you'll remember the time you were far, far away, having a swell time in a Red Light District.

'You're daydreaming again.' Simon dragged me into the shop.

The condoms came in every shape, colour and flavour imaginable. They came looking like animals and people and vehicles and buildings, and they came with spots and spikes and hard bits and soft bits. All very safe and clean and tourist-friendly. I couldn't tell you if they were the same styles as the ones I'd seen here last time. I didn't care much then, and I cared even less now.

It was impossible to connect this Disneyfied nonsense with what I'd just witnessed a street and a half earlier. I couldn't help wondering if my Medusa girl had ever been pumped with a rubberised version of Snow White or Poseidon. Or if, at five euros a pop, these johnnies were too precious to waste on Red Light pussy.

For my ninth birthday I got a Cindy doll. She wore a pink

meringue dress. The sort of dress that, if she were real, and it was still the eighties, she would wear to her high school prom. The sort of dress that, if she were real *now*, would make her look like one of those perfectly pretty but perfectly insane girls, with pencil-thin arms covered in magic-marker-thick scars.

To a nine-year-old, Cindy's look was aspirational. She wasn't as skinny as her cousin Barbie, whose waist was about twenty times smaller than her tits, and whose feet were stuck in eternal tiptoes, making high-heels her only option. Cindy had flat feet. She had a sturdy waist and believable breasts.

For my tenth birthday I got another doll: Paul. He had white teeth, bendable arms, and a shiny jacket. He came with a miniature chocolate box.

I remember the moment Paul and Cindy first met. I made Paul walk up to Cindy, nice and slow. 'For you,' he said, in a deep, sexy voice, holding out the chocolates.

'Thank you,' Cindy simpered. She gazed into Paul's eyes.

I laid the box of chocolates down on the carpet. I undid the zip on Cindy's dress and pulled it carefully over her head. I took off her flat shoes.

I removed Paul's shiny jacket, and pulled down his all-in-one-shirt-and-trouser-suit.

I pressed their bodies together.

I made them kiss like movie stars.

I dropped Paul on the floor.

Somehow, I realised, having Paul there was making me love Cindy less. I took Cindy in both hands, staring intently at her plastic curves, wondering if one day this is what my nipples would grow into. With a small shiver, I lifted Cindy to my mouth, and held one of her curves between my teeth.

Back at the hotel, I slumped on the bed with a beer and a magazine while Simon had a shower. I was exhausted. We must have biked our way around half of Amsterdam.

I wasn't really reading the magazine; just staring at the pictures. I wondered how *I* would look on those glossy pages. If anyone would notice me in there. See that something wasn't right, that one of the women in there wasn't a proper model. It'd be like a game of *Where's Wally?* And I'd be the wally.

Of course people would notice. I was five foot four. The muscle on my upper arms was turning to flab, and I had too many freckles. My hair kinked in weird places, even with straighteners, and I had permanently tired eyes.

I stared at a page consisting entirely of photographs of handbags and wondered what was in store for tonight. I wanted to get drunk. Simon wanted to get stoned and then eat one of those twenty-course Indonesian meals we'd seen advertised everywhere. I'd had one of those when I was last here, then spent the next few hours curled up into a ball. Just me, my irritable bowels, and a world of pain.

But Simon wasn't to know I'd been here before. Nobody knew, actually. Shortly after my dad died, I pulled a sickie. Took three days off work and flew out here on a whim. No reason in particular, other than it was the cheapest holiday online. Since the very first section of my tourist guide was about the Red Light District, that's where I went first. Never strayed any further. Now, several months later, here I was again. And Simon was trying really hard to cheer me up. He just didn't know how.

'Phew, that feels better,' he sighed, wrapped up in one of the hotel's not-so-fluffy-white towels. 'Gretchen,' he said suddenly. 'Are you…?'

I grew aware of myself. Lying on my back, hands in my pants, with the Problem Pages lying open beside me. 'Hey,' I said, 'how about a quickie?'

Simon looked at me, weighing up the pros and cons, I imagine, then he whipped off his towel.

I pushed my fingers deeper into myself and thought about the neon-pink erections we'd seen on the teddy bears in the shop window.

'You look hot,' Simon gasped, falling on top of me.

I took out my fingers and pulled down my pants.

'Oh, hang on a minute.' He jumped off the bed and knelt on the floor. I heard the rustle of plastic, then another sound: like a lid peeling back. It couldn't be, could it? Oh god, no. Not a chocolate box.

'Ta da!' he shouted. 'What do you think?' On the tip of his penis was a bright green crocodile. Its beady eyes were looking straight at me.

'It's great,' I told him, then closed my eyes and let him in.

'Oh, fuck,' he groaned. Sex was the only time Simon ever swore. The rest of the time he was all 'sugar' and 'fiddlesticks' with the occasional 'damn'.

I was always perfectly quiet while having sex with Simon. I just moved quietly and obediently in rhythm with him, and sometimes let my eyes roll back.

'Fucking hell!' he shouted, pushing frantically inside me. Then he stopped and groaned.

Simon was quicker than any man I'd ever known.

'Oh babe,' he panted, pulling out painfully quickly and lying next to me. 'You turn me on *so much*.'

I pulled up my pants. The crocodile had hurt me. I think it might have been for novelty purposes only. 'Yes,' I murmured, running my thumb along one of his bendable arms. 'You too, Paul.'

The next day we took a wrong turn at the park and ended up spending three hours longer on our bikes than planned. By the time we got to the Anne Frank house our day had almost disappeared. This particularly annoyed me, since I'd never made it here on my last visit. After forty-five minutes of queuing, I practically ran up to the attic.

Anne Frank's bedroom.

I spent as long as I possibly could in there. 'She was called Annelies,' I mused. 'I bet most people don't know that.'

Simon was staring at the map, trying to figure out the most efficient way home.

Imagine being cooped up somewhere like this, I kept thinking. Imagine having to be so still, so quiet. Imagine the strange, secret thoughts you'd keep inside you before sleep. Locked away from the world. No windows.

When we left, I bought a keyring so I'd never forget it there.

I haven't forgotten it.

I haven't forgotten about my Medusa girl, either. Now, in my dreams, I refer to her as Anne. Anne Frank with windows.

At night, when I touch myself, I'm never quite sure which Anne I'm thinking of. And I'm even less sure why thinking about either of them should make me feel the way I do.

Borderline

'I think you've got this,' said Simon, handing me a book called *I Hate You – Don't Leave Me*.

'What's that?' I asked, screwing up my nose at the clashing colours and terrible font.

'Borderline Personality Disorder. I think you've got it.'

'Oh,' I said, flicking through the pages but not reading the words.

'Found it on Amazon.' He took the book back. 'I was thinking we could look at it together, see if it helps.'

'Okay.' I pulled the covers down, showing him my breasts, and scrunched a handful of his hair. 'Do you want to have sex?'

'I've got to leave in ten minutes,' he said, patting my left breast. 'The broadband man is due at nine. Plus I need to put some laundry on.' He heaved himself out of bed and chucked the book onto the mattress. As he walked towards the door, I noticed that he didn't have an erection. He never did in the mornings, not any more, but I always looked, just in case.

I picked up the book and skimmed through a few pages, until I saw a list. Apparently there were eight criteria used to diagnose Borderline Personality Disorder. At least five must be present, the book said, to make a diagnosis. The criteria were:

1. *Unstable and intense interpersonal relationships.*
2. *Impulsiveness in potentially self-damaging behaviours, such as substance abuse, sex, shoplifting, reckless driving, binge eating.*
3. *Severe mood shifts.*
4. *Frequent and inappropriate displays of anger.*
5. *Recurrent suicidal threats or gestures, or self-mutilating behaviours.*
6. *Lack of clear sense of identity.*
7. *Chronic feelings of emptiness or boredom.*
8. *Frantic efforts to avoid real or imagined abandonment.*

I threw the book on the floor. What was my boyfriend trying to tell me? That I was a nutcase? That he hated me? That he wanted to break up with me?

He came back into the room in his jeans and t-shirt, carrying his shoes. I always felt a horrible pang when I saw him carrying his shoes.

'Stay for a bit,' I implored him. 'Arrange for the broadband man to come another day. Or tell him you'll be an hour late? You can't just diagnose me with a mental illness and then leave.'

'Keep the book for now,' he said, tying his shoelaces, 'and, if it's nice weather at the weekend, maybe we can take it to the park and discuss it together.'

'Like a baby,' I said.

'What?'

'Nothing.'

He picked up the book and put it on the bedside table, balancing it on top of a precarious pile of novels and short story collections. I was halfway through them all, unable to finish any. He kissed the top of my head. 'I'll see you

Saturday.'

'It's Thursday today.'

'Are you going to get up?'

'I don't know.' I wriggled back under the covers with a frown. 'I might just lie here.'

'Okay, well have a good day.' I heard him picking up his bag. The front door opened and shut.

What a prick, I thought. *What an actual prick.*

Took me ages to find the strength to get out of bed. The sun's glare was becoming increasingly accusatory, until eventually I had no choice but to drag myself out from under the covers.

Aprovecha el momento, as Simon would say.

I took off my pyjamas and dry-brushed my body, particularly my thighs and left arm, where the biggest marks were. My body looked such a mess these days. Badly-drawn tattoos and thick purple scars: the track marks of blades gone by. I had a hot shower, then rubbed an expensive vitamin-filled oil over my skin, which made the scars very shiny but I'm not convinced it reduced them in any way. The hopelessness of it all made me want to cut myself again, but I didn't. Instead, I pulled on a tracksuit, because I felt too frumpy to wear a dress, and I sat on my sofa, looking out of the window.

I should do something, I thought.

It was now almost a year since my dad had died. I had quit my job and was living off my dwindling inheritance: the money I was meant to be saving for a mortgage, or my wedding day, or a round-the-world trip, or my first-born child – and here it was, disappearing on gas bills and baked beans, as I sat listening to time pass.

I opened my laptop. Instead of looking at the screen, I watched the people out in the street for a bit, moving from the left side of the window to the right, from the right side of the window to the left. As I watched them, a tiny question popped into my mind. A tiny, persistent question, that I asked myself almost every day.

What does it feel like to be normal?

Finally, I looked at the computer screen. Perhaps I could become addicted to a new game. Like the time I played out the existence of my alter ego, Jake. That could while away a few days.

But I didn't do that. I opened a blank document and made a list.

Epilator
Cabbages
Rice cakes
Ulysses
Eye shadow

I liked making lists, especially shopping lists. The best bit was ticking the items off one by one until they were done. Sometimes I employed a special double technique. First I'd tick them to show I was about to embark on them, and then I'd put a line through them to show they were finished. It was very satisfying, all that achieving. Tick, line, done. Tick, line, done.

Now I'd made the list I felt better. I needed an epilator to shave my underarms and legs – an alternative to razors, since Simon had banished them from my flat. Cabbages (lots) for this new diet I wanted to try. Rice cakes, because the cabbage diet sounded disgusting. *Ulysses* because I was embarrassed to call myself an English Literature graduate when I'd never read Joyce's seminal work. And eye shadow, because I'd overheard someone saying that purple shadow on blue eyes made your eyes look like they were going to 'pop'. I wanted my eyes to 'pop'. Maybe Simon would want to have sex with me if my eyes 'popped'.

After another hour of faffing, printing out my list, drinking tea, picking at the dry skin on my feet, I left the house.

Once I'd bought the stuff, and had a list full of ticks and lines, I decided to walk the long way home. The sun was still shining and I felt buoyant. I swung the carrier bags containing my purchases, smiling at the pedestrians who were smiling, avoiding the glances of the ones that looked anxious. I bought myself a chocolate bar, just as a treat, to try and boost the feeling. Then I bought myself a bottle of wine, and thought how nice it would be to go home, open the window, listen to some music and drink. I might even dance.

So that is what I did. Except a car alarm kept going off out in the street, so I had to shut the window, and either I was drinking the wine too fast, or the cabbage soup wasn't soaking it up properly, because I was pissed by four. Still, I had an amazing time. I danced on the table to a shitload of nineties grunge, cackling now and again at the brilliance of it all, watching the people out on the street, going left to right, right to left, and I marvelled at the fact that they'd never know what it was like to feel like me, to be this exuberant, this happy with the world, with everything.

What does it feel like to be normal? Who cares!

At eight o'clock I had a little cry, then gave my boyfriend five missed calls before finally cleaning my teeth and going to bed. In bed, I contemplated suicide for around two minutes, then passed out.

The next day I woke early. I had that rushing feeling I get in my body the morning after drinking. Quickened heartbeat, restless legs, panicky throb in my stomach. That's the way I feel most mornings.

I rolled over and looked at the books on the bedside table. *Ulysses* was big. Impossibly big. The mental illness one, *Don't Hate Me – I'm Leaving You*, or whatever it was called, was the thinnest book on the pile.

There is my project for today, I thought. *I'm going to read that book.*

But first, I decided, I would get out of bed, go and make a strong mug of coffee. Shake off the hangover.

In the kitchen, I had a better idea. I looked at my phone, which had a text message from Simon sent at nine-thirty last night, apologising for missing my calls, and then another at ten asking if I was okay. I called him.

'Morning!' I said. 'Hope I didn't wake you.'

'It's okay, I was just up quite late getting this track finished.' His voice was croaky; I wanted to cuddle him.

'I'm making pancakes,' I squealed. 'Do you want to come over?' I whisked up some batter, holding the phone between my ear and shoulder as I spoke.

He coughed. 'I think I'm going to sleep a bit more,' he said, 'I've got a late shift tonight.'

'I could wait for an hour? Leave the batter to stand in

the fridge? Actually, it's better that way.'

'What time is it?'

'Half eight. Nearly a quarter to nine.'

He groaned. 'I'll call you in an hour,' he said. 'Love you.'

'Love you too.' I hung up and looked at the mess I'd made. I went back to the bedroom, muttering under my breath, then got into bed.

There, something amazing happened. I picked up the book and began to read. Now when I say read, here's the thing. I'm not very good at reading when I'm stressed. I can still read words, sentences even, but they're not linear. I'll often open a book somewhere in the middle, then read the last paragraph of a page, then jump back to the previous one, then again, all the way to the start of the page. I don't know why that is. It doesn't help with the stress. If anything, it makes it worse.

So today, when I picked up the book, I opened the book somewhere in the middle, flicked back a few pages until I found the diagnostic criteria again, and I re-read the final point on the list, number eight.

8. Frantic efforts to avoid real or imagined abandonment.

I couldn't work out what it meant. Abandonment? I pictured a newborn kitten, shivering in an alleyway. How did that relate to me? No one had ever abandoned me. My parents had done all they could to care for me. In my twenty-eight years on this planet, I had never even been dumped. My friends always used to say they thought it would be good for me, to get well and truly dumped. A taste of my own medicine. But I'd never given anyone the chance. I'd ended every single relationship I'd ever had. Some of those endings had been mutual, no doubt, but I'd still been the instigator. How many relationships had I ended, in that case? Twenty? Thirty? Forty? Maybe more. And that's just the proper ones, by which I mean anyone I would introduce publicly as my 'boyfriend'. Or girlfriend, but I'd never quite managed one of them.

I skipped forwards a couple of pages, and read:

Promiscuity often expresses a need for constant love and attention from others, in order to hold on to positive feelings about oneself.

And:

romantic attachments are highly-charged and usually short-lived. The borderline will frantically pursue a man (or woman) one day and send him packing the next. Longer romances – usually measured in weeks or months rather than years – are usually filled with turbulence and rage, wonder and excitement.

Then I skipped back a bit:

Sustained periods of contentment are foreign to the borderline. Chronic emptiness eats at him until he is forced to do anything in order to escape.

I couldn't help it after that. I was hopping all over the place.

The world of a borderline, like that of a child, is split into heroes and villains.

...

Lacking a core sense of identity, borderlines commonly experience a painful loneliness that motivates them to find ways to fill up the 'holes'.

...

The borderline is... a cultural amnesiac; his cupboard of warm memories (which sustain most of us in troubled times) is bare. As a result, he is doomed to suffer torment with no breathers, no concrete memories of happier times to get him through the tough periods. Unable to learn from his mistakes, he is doomed to repeat them.

My phone rang. 'Simon.'

'Babe. Sorry about earlier. I was exhausted. Fancy getting a bite to eat?'

'Sure. Pancakes?'

'I was thinking we could go out. It's nearly lunchtime now anyway.'

'Oh, okay.' I pictured the mess in my kitchen, and felt glad to be able to close the door on it until later.

'Meet you at Café Rio in half an hour?'

'Done.' I put the book in my bag, had a shower, epilated my legs and underarms, then applied a thick line of purple to each eyelid.

Wearing a dress and make-up, I felt great as I walked in, and I couldn't quite believe how handsome Simon looked, sitting there waiting for me with his unkempt hair, his tight blue jumper, and a newspaper on the table in front of him. Here was the man I loved. Here was the man I would risk everything for.

'How are you doing?' he asked as I sat down.

I looked at my hands. I tried to say the word 'good', but felt a bit funny all of a sudden. I had my back to the room. The sunlight was streaming on my face. My eyes felt stupid. Were they 'popping'? Who wanted their eyes to pop anyway? I once knew a woman with a thyroid problem; her eyes looked like they were going to pop.

'I'm starving,' said Simon.

He ordered Eggs Benedict and I ordered Eggs Florentine. He ordered orange juice and I ordered coffee.

'Do you want to swap places?' he asked when we sat back down. 'I know you like to face the room.'

I nodded, thanked him, and began to feel better again. 'Do you remember that story?' I asked, taking his hand. 'The one I wrote after we had an argument? That day we listened to the radio play, then we had a row and you went home?'

'The one about an imaginary lover?'

'That's the one. In the story, my imaginary lover and I listen to a radio play, just like you and I did in real life, but in the story, my lover and I don't have an argument – we have a bath – and then we leave the flat together and go to a café.'

'Yes, I remember.'

'When I wrote it, I imaged that *this* was the café in that story.'

'Café Rio?'

'Yes.'

Our drinks arrived and we let go of each other's hands.

Simon peered at me over the top of his cup. 'Did you read any of that book I gave you?'

'Hang on a minute, I was trying to tell you something,' I protested.

'Sorry, I didn't realise. Carry on.'

'I've forgotten now. I don't know. Something about that story, and us, and that day we spent together. I guess the story was an apology.'

'For what?'

'For the argument.'

'I see.' He took a sip of juice, and I knew that he didn't see.

'Anyway,' I said, just as our eggs arrived, 'I did read some of the book. I've got it here now.' I motioned towards my bag.

'What do you think?'

'I think you have Asperger's Syndrome,' I replied. This wasn't the reply I was expecting to give. It had been a thought I'd been forming for the past few months, and it just escaped, there and then.

'Asperger's? Why?'

'Well,' I said slowly. 'My sister has it. I think my dad had it. I think you have it.'

'Are you saying this because you're upset about the book?'

'No. I'm saying it because you live inside your own head too much. You're obsessed with music. You can be really tactless sometimes and you have no idea when it comes to social conventions.' I could feel my cheeks burning. My anger made the egg taste horrible.

'I don't think I have Asperger's,' he said, 'but let's talk about it some more. Maybe we could discuss it in the park tomorrow, when we talk about your condition. The forecast is good.'

'Forecast for what?' I asked moronically, then I didn't talk for the rest of the meal.

The longer I stayed silent, the surer I felt that this relationship wasn't going to last. I just couldn't envisage a future with someone so thoughtless. What was he doing giving me a book on Borderline Personality Disorder anyway? Who did he think he was: a psychiatrist? I'd seen enough of *them* in my time – useless waste of space, the lot of them. Besides, none of them had ever mentioned Borderline Personality Disorder before.

After the meal, I put my money on the table and walked out. Simon settled the bill and rushed after me. 'Look,' he said, 'Sorry if I've upset you. Can we talk about it?'

'Fuck off,' I told him. 'It's over.'

'I really want to talk about it,' he said. 'I've got to go to the studio today. Get this track mastered. The album's almost finished, you know. But I've put you in the diary for tomorrow. We can spend the whole day together.'

'Tomorrow is too late,' I spat. 'Leave me alone.'

And he did, and I hated him even more for it.

When I got back to the flat, I got my gym things together. I ran ten kilometres on the treadmill and developed a stitch, exercising so soon after food. Then I came home and collapsed on the sofa. I'm pathetic, I said to myself. I don't know what I'm doing.

I ate all the cabbage soup, then all the rice cakes, then I drank a four-pack of beer. I left seven messages on Simon's phone: four of them furious, two of them apologetic, one of them livid. Then I texted my ex-boyfriend and told him I was touching myself. He didn't reply.

At half-past seven, Simon called and asked if I wanted to go to a concert.

'Where have you been all day?' I asked.

'In the studio, like I said I would be. The reception's rubbish.'

'Are you lying?'

'No, course not. So what do you think? It's Brahms.'

I chewed my fingernails, looked at my hair in the mirror: disastrous. 'What time does it start?'

'Eight. Meet you in town in twenty minutes?'

'Fine.'

I got ready in three minutes flat and went to listen to some Brahms.

I guess I was a bit drunk, but I found the music boring. It didn't make me feel the surge I'd felt while listening to Rachmaninoff, or the sparkle I'd felt on first hearing Debussy. The orchestra were thrusting away at their violins like they were getting off on it, and I didn't feel a thing. I clenched my hand in a fist.

Simon looked at me as the music was playing and blinked. One, two, three. It was a trick I'd taught him: a *cat kiss*, I called it. My sister and I gave them to each other to show affection instead of touching. Blink-blink-blinkety-blink. Simon was trying to tell me he loved me, and here I was making a fist.

The music ended. On the way out of the auditorium, Simon asked what I'd thought of the concert. 'Seven out of ten,' I said. 'You?'

'Pretty good,' he replied, but I guessed he was holding back for my benefit somehow.

'Fancy a drink?' I asked.

'Yeah.'

We went to the pub directly opposite the City Halls, got ourselves a couple of beers, and I felt a bit more relaxed again. The stereo was playing one of my favourite songs, an electronica tune with romantic lyrics.

Halfway through my second pint, I said: 'I'm sorry, Simon. I think we're from different worlds. When you listen to Brahms, you're thinking about time signatures or scales or chromatics, or something. But do you know what I was thinking about?'

'No. What?' He put his hand on my leg, moved it up an inch towards my knickers. It was unintentional.

I put my hand over his, holding it there so it wouldn't slide back down. 'I imagined I was watching *A Clockwork Orange*. One of those scenes of ultra-violence, where all that classical music is played over the top of a big fight, and there's blood spraying everywhere.'

He looked down at the table, then back at me. 'That was Beethoven,' he said. 'Not Brahms.'

We finished our beers, then went back to his place, the place we used to live together, before the break-up, and I lay beside him in the spare room. Not the room we used to sleep in, the room I'd painted for us, the room we'd built our bed in – *that* room he was now renting out to a fellow musician. We lay in the spare room, squashed together on the single bed, my forehead pressed against the wall, and it all got a bit much for me. At three o'clock in the morning, I left.

The next day we met in the park as planned. I didn't bother with eye shadow today, but I did wear a dress. A white one, with ribbons at the collar. It was an *I'm sorry* dress, all innocence and naivety. I needed him to think I was a nice person, because, essentially, I was.

'I've got the book with me.' I sat on the grass beside him. 'Shall we talk about it?'

'Actually,' he said, 'I went back on Amazon and read some reviews. The book I gave you was written during the eighties. Some of the ideologies are a bit... old-fashioned. Here. These ones got the most five stars.'

He handed me two new books with boring titles. They looked so sombre. So not me.

'And I got this too.' He handed me a third book: *All About Asperger's*. 'I'm open to your suggestion,' he said, with a smile. It was a really lovely smile too. I kissed him full on the lips.

He pulled away. 'Let's get started,' he said, opening the thicker of the two books.

This book mentioned *nine* diagnostic criteria for BPD. The new addition to the list was:

9. Transient, stress-related paranoid ideation or severe dissociative symptoms.

It went on to quote from this thing called DSM-IV, which refers to the fourth edition of some textbook called the *Diagnostic and Statistical Manual of Mental Disorders*:

The essential feature of Borderline Personality Disorder

is a pervasive pattern of instability of interpersonal relationships, self-image, and affects, and marked impulsivity that begins by early adulthood and is present in a variety of contexts.

'What do you think?' Simon asked. 'Do you identify with any of the symptoms?'

'A bit, I suppose. Most of them. Yeah, all of them, I guess.'

'Even the one about paranoid ideation?'

'Mm-hmm.'

'Which one do you identify with the most?'

'I don't know,' I said. 'Look, it's not a fucking shopping list, is it? It's complicated.' I ran my eyes down the numbers, giving each criterion a mental tick, then putting a line through it. Tick, line, done. Tick, line, done.

'So there isn't one in particular you feel applies to you more than the others?

'I don't know. Maybe the one about unstable relationships. Ours hasn't exactly been the smoothest. But then since we've been going out, so much has happened. My sister keeps trying to kill herself. My dad died. Mum went AWOL. Anyone would find it difficult to be stable in those conditions.'

'True.'

'Anyone with half a brain would be diagnosed with severe depression in that scenario, and would have to go on tablets like me.'

'Maybe.'

'There was the time my block of flats caught fire and I got Post-Traumatic Stress Disorder. You'd have to be *an idiot* not to be affected by something like that.'

'Perhaps.'

'And then when I read your diary, and saw all the things you'd written about those other girls…'

Simon held me and began stroking my forehead. He did this whenever I got upset, and it always calmed me down. 'I'm sorry,' he whispered. 'I want to help you.'

I took a deep breath and nestled under his arm. 'I guess it must be much more difficult for you than it is for me,' I told him. 'All the things I've done.' Then we worked through the book, paragraph by paragraph.

Simon pointed to the page. 'This bit's interesting. Borderline Personality Disorder sufferers tend to have less boundaries than other people. It can lead to them being incredibly honest and open, sometimes leading to what others might see as a bit of an *overshare*.'

'I don't do that, do I?'

'Oh look. It also says that people with BPD often engage in something called *splitting*, which means they tend to see things in black and white. So they view people as either "good" or "bad", and can switch from one to the other very quickly.'

'Heroes and villains.'

'Some sufferers may idolise one figure in particular, someone who is unlikely to abandon them, a family member or a friend. Someone they can fall back on when times are hard.'

I picked a bit of grass and sprinkled it onto my knee. There was a family playing Frisbee further down the hill. An endless circle of spin and catch. Mummy, Daddy, son, daughter. Nuclear. Perfect. I wished I had a baby. I wished I could catch.

'Well? Don't you think that sounds familiar?'

'Maybe,' I said quietly.

'That's how you saw your dad.'

I raised my eyebrows.

'When he died, he abandoned you.'

'Well he hardly did it on purpose,' I said, sprinkling more grass on my knee, noticing that my voice had become higher-pitched, more childlike.

'So *that's* why you've been grieving so badly!' His eyes lit up. 'I think I understand you now.'

I wiped the grass off my knee. 'When are we going to get started on the Asperger's book? It's getting late.'

Simon put down the book and held me again, stroking my head. 'We can get through this.'

'You don't know if I've got it,' I said. 'This is all total conjecture. I could have any number of things. Or nothing. You're no doctor.'

'Will you see one?'

'I don't know.'

'Try?'

'Maybe.'

Not long after that, we walked back to my flat, arm in arm. I felt calmer than I had done in a while, especially since I knew that we still had a whole evening left together, and that he'd be there beside me in the morning. It sounds silly, but feeling his heartbeat, the warmth of his skin next to mine, it helped me feel alive.

That night we made spaghetti, then we made love. It was good sex, very normal sex, first me on top, then a bit of missionary, and I didn't feel like I wanted him to pin me down or hurt me this time. I was happy for the whole thing to be peaceful, sensual, full of love.

Afterwards we watched a Woody Allen film. It was a fake documentary about a guy who transforms himself, in both his looks and his manners, to mirror anyone he is nearby.

'You do that a bit,' Simon said, still stroking my head. I began to wonder if this was some sort of medical technique he'd learnt on the internet, if perhaps he was stroking some particular lobe in my head, some nodule or cortex, that rendered me instantly affable.

'Do what?' I asked in my little girl voice.

'You change all the time, depending on who you're with.'

'Everyone does,' I said, and we left it at that.

Once the film was over, I promised Simon that I would go and see a doctor. I didn't know if anything would come of it, I said, and I didn't know if I actually had this condition or not, and if I did then it might even be mixed with lots of other things, and maybe *I* had a touch of Asperger's too, and maybe I was bipolar, and maybe we *both* had a little bit of everything, maybe everyone did, maybe it was just something intrinsic in Western society, or all society, and even if I did have Borderline Personality Disorder it didn't make me a bad person, and there was some stuff about the condition that was good anyway, like living without boundaries and being open to new things, but my god, there really have been certain patterns of behaviour I've repeated again and again throughout my life that have caused me enormous amounts of hurt and harm, and thank you for being so understanding about it all, and please don't hate me, and please don't leave me, and–

Just before he left the next day, Simon took something out of his bag. 'Here,' he said, and I felt it, the horrible weight of it in my hand. What now? Schizophrenia? Histrionic Behaviour? Obsessive Compulsive Disorder?

Actually, no. It was a CD.

'I've finished it,' he said. 'My album. I really hope you like it.'

'Wow, thanks.'

He kissed me. 'Last night was good,' he said, grinning. 'One to remember, eh?'

It took me a moment to realise he was talking about sex, then I flashed a smile back. 'Yeah.'

'I'll read the Asperger's book,' he told me. 'We'll talk about it on Tuesday.'

'Tuesday. Right. I'll phone the doctors today,' I said. 'And maybe even read *Ulysses*.'

Then he was out of the door.

I wanted to open the door and run down the stairwell after him, screaming that I loved him. But I didn't. I didn't phone the doctor either. I went straight to my laptop and put in the CD, plugged in my speakers, and waited.

I listened to the album all the way through, twice, and I couldn't believe it. Every song was about us.

Simon was singing about what I've put him through, how much he loves me, how sad I've made him, how worried he is, how much of himself he has had to sacrifice to be with me.

I cried when I first heard it, but on second listening I felt quite different. I felt euphoric. Perfectly, madly euphoric, that at last he had been able to let it all out.

For Anyone Who Wants To Be Friends With Me

If you are considering being friends with me, there are a few things you ought to know.

I like springtime, dancing, blueberries, and linguistics.

I don't like frogs, polystyrene balls, hairdressers, or lies.

Once, I won a trophy for excellence in music.

Another time, this happened.

It was Christmas Eve. I worked in Our Price (remember it?). One day I got graded 27% by a secret shopper. The report said: 'friendly but ignorant'. I was fine with that.

So, Christmas Eve. We had to listen to festive songs all day, and answer questions from grannies holding long lists of band names they didn't know. 'Napalm Death? For your grandson?' I'd say to some old dear. 'Certainly, Madam. Right this way.' And she and her Zimmer frame would follow close behind, while Noddy Holder blared from the speakers above me.

After an exhausting day's work, I went back to a friend's house. We'd been talking about lesbianism for some time now (it all started with a drunken heart-to-heart in the Wetherspoons toilets) and I wondered if tonight might be the night I'd finally kiss her. Didn't fancy her or anything, but there comes a time when you've talked about something for so long you start to think you actually want it.

In her bedroom we drank vodka. We peeled off our red Our Price sweaters, taking small sideways glances at each other's underwear as we put on our party gear. I wore a miniskirt, fishnet tights, and a black shirt covered in homemade glitter-glue slogans. Scrawled in silver across my shoulder blades was 'broken wings'. I gelled my lilac hair into perfect spikes, applied even more black eye make-up than I wore to work, tightened my piercings, and away we went into the night.

I was barely eighteen; still too young to wear a coat. It was freezing, but the drink helped.

We went to a pub in Buckingham and drank a lot of whisky. After that, another pub, more drink. I don't know if you've ever been to Buckingham, but it's not exactly known for its cultural diversity. It's all ferrets, 4x4s and jodhpurs. The 'punk look' tends to stand out. It wasn't uncommon for people to throw things, spit at my face, or shout obscenities as I passed. In this particular pub, we started getting comments off a group of people by the pool table, so we went somewhere else. And drank more whisky.

It was getting pretty late and we were getting pretty drunk, but we still hadn't kissed. I decided to bring it up. 'What do you think would happen if we started kissing, right now, at this table?'

She looked hazily around the room: at the guys fiddling with their phones, at the girls rifling through their handbags, and at the impatient throng, red-faced at the bar.

Then she eyed me.

I have to say, kissing her wasn't as exciting as I hoped it would be. It was small and warm and like any other mouth

I'd ever stuck my tongue in. Couldn't even feel her lip piercing, so I doubt whether she could feel mine.

Seconds into the kiss, I felt a tap on my shoulder.

'Hey girls,' slurred someone whose face has, in my memory, vanished. 'You should come with us.' He motioned towards the guy in the rugby shirt beside him.

Drunk and intrigued, we got up from our table. We held hands and followed the man and his friend.

There was only one cubicle in the men's loos. I remember thinking that was weird, but I guess men aren't shy unless they're taking a shit. The four of us bundled in, and the men locked the door and told us to kiss again. We felt their hands run over us, sliding under our tops, grabbing our bums.

I could hear Noddy Holder in the room next door. The same song I'd been listening to all day at work.

So here it is…

With one sharp tug, my tights were pulled down, and I felt a hard, wet lump of flesh being squeezed into me.

Everybody's having fun…

'Bend over', said a gruff voice, as I was pushed over the cistern. I grasped the toilet seat to steady myself while he grabbed at my glitter glue, ripping apart my 'broken wings'.

From the sound of things, my friend was getting banged against the cubicle door.

It's about this point that my memory gets very, very cloudy indeed.

I remember thinking that I didn't want to be here, and I can just about remember the sea of faces hanging over the top of the cubicle: at least half a dozen of them, stinking of beer and sweat and aftershave. Cheering.

Meanwhile, the cock inside me came.

Then another cock came inside me.

And another.

The faces hanging over the top of the cubicle changed places, and we were fucked by man after man. My clothes got ripped. My thighs dripped with semen.

'Get out!' screamed a voice – a woman's voice – somewhere outside the cubicle. 'What the fuck do you think you're doing? Get the fuck out of here! You're barred.'

I wasn't sure who was barred exactly, because there were so many of us in there, but I knew I wouldn't be going back to that pub ever again. I kept my eyes on the carpet as I walked back through the busy bar and out into the street.

I could feel the cold more than ever now. The whole of me was stinging. My friend and I didn't say a word. We gripped each other's hands, zigzagging the pavement back towards her house.

'Hey, wait!' someone called out. 'Don't you want to come with us for a Christmas drink?'

We stopped.

There were two men behind us. It was hard to tell whether they had been in the loos with us or not. I was having trouble remembering anything at that point.

My friend let go of my hand. 'I could do with a drink,' she said.

While she walked ahead with one of the guys, the other

took his place beside me. They led us down an alleyway.

'Stop,' urged the guy with me. He pushed me up against a wheelie bin. It was a quick and awkward fuck, and he didn't utter a thing until afterwards, when he called me a 'dirty bitch'.

We caught up with the others.

'This is my car,' said one of them. 'Let's get in.' My friend and her guy got in the front, me and mine in the back. There isn't really a polite way to say what happened next.

They fucked. We fucked.

The guys swapped seats and we swapped fucks.

My friend crawled into the back with me and the men told us to lick each other out. She sat on the seat and – I don't know how I did it – but somehow I went upside down, and I did her while she did me, vertical.

Then we went into a house.

I got in a bed, in a different room to my friend. I lay as still as I could until it was over, then it dawned on me that it was Christmas Eve. I called a taxi.

'Where are you going?' asked the guy.

'Home,' I said.

About twenty minutes later I stumbled out of the taxi and stood swaying at my front gate. At the gate was my mother.

'Hi, Mum.'

'Where the hell have you been?' she screamed. 'I've called the police!'

'Just out. I'm fine.'

'Why are your tights around your neck?'

I looked down and noticed my legs were bare. My fishnets were wrapped around my neck. 'I fell in a puddle,'

I slurred.

'Get inside.'

The last thing I remember thinking before I fell asleep is that I had lost my knickers.

My sister ran into my room at 6 a.m. 'It's Christmaaaas!' I pulled the duvet over my face.

We sat in the lounge to unwrap our presents: me, Lottie, my mum, my dad. Mum scowled as I opened my gifts. I alternated between saying thank you and running upstairs to be sick, too groggy to register the hair slides, socks, and perfume I'd been given.

At 7 a.m, we got in the car and started the two-hour drive to my uncle's. We were spending Christmas with him this year because he was alone and had Parkinson's. The whole journey, I listened to Slade on the stereo as I held in the vomit.

It's only just begu-u-un...

When we arrived, I ran into the bathroom and threw up. I went to bed and missed Christmas dinner.

My grandparents were at my uncle's too. When I finally got up, Granddad laughed. 'Your mummy tells me you had fun last night.' I nodded, running my hands through my lilac hair, hoping that my Deftones hoodie hid the bruises. I went into the kitchen for a glass of water and a cry.

We sat in the living room watching old re-runs of *Only Fools and Horses*, eating cheese and biscuits. My uncle drank his wine through a straw because only a quarter of his face was working.

At some point that evening I got a text.

merry xmas from paul

I didn't remember giving out my number.

When Paul asked me out on a date a few days later, I said yes. I thought it might normalise things. Cancel out the other night, if we could manage to have a nice time. We had a chat: he was twenty-one, worked in Sainsbury's, liked snooker, hated the dentist. We went to the cinema to see *Road Trip* then drove back to his. I had to run up the stairs so his flatmates wouldn't see me. We had sex. Dry, difficult sex, and then I got up to leave. Before I left, I asked if he had my knickers.

He took them out of his bedside drawer, but said that he wanted to keep them.

'Why?' I asked.

'To smell.'

I snatched them off him. Back at home, I took them out of my coat pocket and stared in horror. Black satin, silver hearts, white stains. I pushed them deep inside the kitchen bin. Then I deleted Paul's number from my phone. Finally, I felt a bit better.

As for my friend, the surprising thing is that I can't remember what happened to her. I guess we must have texted each other, maybe even worked another shift together, but I've honestly forgotten all about it. In fact, I'd forgotten about the whole thing until several years later, when it came back to me in a flash so violent I could hardly breathe.

But after that Christmas Eve, I did other things.

I fucked someone who professed to be a Nazi, I fucked someone on the bathroom floor while he told me he'd 'deflowered a thirteen-year-old', I fucked someone while he told me about his lovely wife and three children, I pissed all over someone while I fucked him, I fucked someone whose dad fed me ketamine, I fucked someone who published a novel in which I was the cruel heroine, I fucked someone who gave me chlamydia, and I fucked myself up, time and time again, because it's all I knew how to do.

Nowadays, my hair is brown and I have pinpricks where my piercings used to be.

There is no glitter glue in my wardrobe. I grow my own herbs and listen to jazz and drink herbal tea and read books about the universe and work hard at my job and laugh at puns and dream about owning a house and kittens and learning to use a sewing machine and travelling to beautiful places. I like springtime and dancing and linguistics.

If you become my friend, I will cook you a meal using fresh coriander. I'll play you Thelonius Monk and offer you a peppermint tea. I'll talk to you about pets and the universe. I'll tell you the link between blueberries and memory loss, if you ask nicely.

But I probably won't tell you any of the other stuff.

Every now and then, though, we'll be sitting in the sunshine, and I'll be in the middle of laughing at your puns, or telling you about all the beautiful places I want to run away to, when I'll stop–

–to look down at my bare legs.

And I'll still feel the fishnets coiled around my neck.

I thought you should know.

Imagine If You Could Run As Fast As This

I overheard this kid on the tram into Manchester the other morning.

Look how fast we're going, he said to his daddy. He hummed under his breath, then his small grey mittens tapped his daddy's shoulder. *I bet I could run this fast*, he declared, then a moment later: *I bet I could run faster than this.*

When I heard that thought process it made me smile, because the boy was just a boy, and the tram was a tram, and people will never run as fast as machines.

Every morning, I arrive at the station just after nine. I'm always later than I meant to be, and I'm always listening to music to forget how late I am. I listen to one of two playlists, depending on my mood. The first playlist is called *Faves Of Outstanding Beauty*. The second is called *Faves With Extra Sauce*. I named the lists myself. The names make me feel a bit sick.

Sometimes I look out of the tram window on the way to work. There's this electronic sign near Deansgate. It has a picture of a turkey on it. On Tuesday, above the turkey, it said *In Six Days We Cook*. I'm guessing on Tuesday there were six days left until Christmas. I think it's supposed to be a play on *In God We Trust*. Somehow the turkey is God, and cooking is our religion.

I'm an atheist.

Normally I arrive at work at 9.36. I try to arrive at different times, but I almost always arrive at 9.36.

The first thing I do when I get to the office is go to the kitchen. I pour myself a coffee, which the permanent staff jokingly refer to as Rocket Fuel. The temporary staff drink so much it hurts.

Three out of seven of the temporary staff are underweight. I am not underweight. But I am temporary.

On the way to work, I sometimes think: what if this is it? What if *this* is the world? Just this strip of space I can see on the way from home into work, and from work back home – what if *this* is everything? These are the only streets, the only cafés, the only job centres, the only canal-side gastropubs, the only churches. And these are the only people.

Most of the time, I find this thought reassuring.

Yesterday was Wednesday. The electronic sign said *In Five Days We Cook*.

Before lunch, I shredded fifty-three sheets of paper. After lunch, I printed out ninety-five sheets. I said hello to eight people. I received two emails about weight loss methods that could change my life. I ate a cheese sandwich out of a tupperware box. I didn't get a single text message.

The first thing I do when I get home is go to the kitchen. I pour myself a glass of wine, just the one, which normally turns into two, then five. The Rocket Fuel will always take the edge off the hangover.

Twice a week I meet up with a married woman I know. We talk about her husband and her children and how she hasn't got time to hear herself think. We talk about how much better life was before it got like this. We talk about all the things we regret. We talk about all the things that make us sad. We kiss when we say goodbye.

Apparently, in four days we cook.

On the mornings after I've met up with the married woman, I can smell her perfume on my skin. It makes me feel ashamed. And aroused.

I often wish I believed in God.

This morning, I was waiting at the coffee machine, and I remembered that little boy on the tram, the one with the grey mittens. *I bet I could run this fast*, he'd announced to his daddy. *I bet I could run faster than this.*

And I remembered that what he'd said that day had made me smile. *Silly boy*, I'd thought, *to think he could go that fast. To think he could go faster than this.*

Today, as I helped myself to a fourth cup of Rocket Fuel, thinking about that little boy made me feel different. It made me feel disappointed. Disappointed because I'm thirty now, and I can't remember the last time I imagined I could run as fast as anything.

The Snow Octopus Who Was
Afraid of the Dark

*This is a story about a snow octopus. No, it's not. It's about a shark
and a football. Some swimming goggles and a diamond ring.*
I've got a better idea. Let me start again.
It was raining for fifteen years in North Korea.

Harry is twice my age, but half as happy. On his walls
he hangs diagrams of poisonous spiders. I've never seen
them because I've never been to his flat. That's one of the
main reasons we're still friends; we've never slept together.
We tried once, if I'm being honest, by a lake at midnight.
But we were drunk, fell asleep, and woke up shivering at 4
a.m. with our trousers round our ankles.

Harry is an actor. Two failed marriages and a failed
career behind him. He likes to go out with older women
and younger men. He collects mental images, like spider
diagrams.

Sometimes Harry imparts the details of his encounters
for several hours at a time. I've worked out that the
description of one encounter takes Harry the exact length
of time it takes me to drink one pint. If we're drinking
wine instead of beer, the descriptions move faster. Harry
never repeats himself. He's had enough encounters to last
a lifetime.

I'm not sure that all the things he tells me are true.

The reason the woman was so sad, so very awkward within her own skin, is because she had never owned a dog.

Ever since her tenth birthday, when she had put 'puppy' on her Christmas list, and instead received a tennis racquet, she had pined for a golden labrador.

She once played at Wimbledon, but even that didn't matter.

Harry has a problem with cocaine. We're all like this, in our circle of friends. We've all got something.

Problems with coke, problems with sex, problems with aggression, with sugar. Some problems are less problematic than others. We have a friend called Colin, for instance, who is addicted to fruit machines. This has led to him becoming remarkably rich. He always was the lucky one.

Harry's problem with coke is serious. It turns him into a jerk and gives him terrible comedowns. I once pretended I'd sourced him a new dealer, and fed him talcum powder for two days. Nosebleeds meant I had to stop.

Today Harry is on The Worst Comedown Ever. We've taken him to a pub in the West End. Today, though, he doesn't want to tell us about his encounters. Today all he wants to do is greet his eyes out.

Richard the Rabbit liked playing poker. He didn't just like it. He loved it. He would go to his friend Rachel's house every Friday night, and they would play together. Once, he was on such a bad losing streak that he had to give away his own tail.

This is how it happened.

We're at a picnic table outside the Belgian bar in Ashton Lane. It's packed with students and arty types, swigging imported beer out of plastic cups, talking about films they're making, singers they're fucking, papers they're writing, and pieces of the world they're going to take over.

I'm drinking a Delirium Tremens with my tattoos on display, and today I feel like I belong.

Colin is a graphic designer who reads a lot of *Batman* in his spare time. He's brought some story dice with him. If you've ever been out with a comic book geek, you might have seen them. There are seven dice in the pack, and each die has a different picture on every side. That's forty-two different pictures. That's a lot of different combinations. The rules are: roll the dice, line them up in a row, and create a story using the pictures in the order they appear.

Colin's girlfriend, Jen, is a painter. She has a problem with aggression, so we tend to let her talk for the longest. She's telling a story about a ship in a storm. Most of her stories involve ships in storms, one way or another.

Harry is half-listening to Jen, and half-looking at his phone, greeting his eyes out. I give Harry's foot a tap under the table. 'Another drink?'

The ship creaked and rocked from side to side. The crew slid from port to starboard, starboard to port, holding on to the edges for dear life. The storm was forecast for another six days.

I hand Harry a gin and get stuck in to my next Delirium. A girl on the grassy slope is watching me. She's wearing a maxi dress and I wonder if she has any cuts on her legs like me. I wonder if she likes to kiss other girls. I wonder if she enjoys standing on mountaintops, screaming.

'Harry,' I whisper, trying not to distract Jen. 'I think I have a personality problem.'

For the first time today, Harry looks up and smiles. His front teeth are grey. 'We all have a personality problem, darling.'

'No,' I say quietly. 'Borderline Personality Disorder. I think I've got it.' I put my hand on his. 'The thing you were diagnosed with last autumn.'

Something shifts behind Harry's eyes and he looks back at his phone. We all have diagnoses, we are all sensitive about them, we all hate them, and we all want exclusive rights to them.

'You don't want that,' he says to his Samsung Galaxy. 'No, you don't want BPD. Get something else.'

Currently I'm the one in our group with the most boring diagnosis. Severe depression. I must have something more exciting than that.

At night, the magical fox didn't have a care in the world. He rooted in bins, smacked his lips at vixens, and bared his teeth as he prowled chicken coops.

But during the day, those long hours of light were torture. Those were the loneliest hours of his life.

'Look,' Harry says, handing me his phone. He's opened a website entitled *Famous People With BPD*. 'Read it aloud,' he instructs.

'Okay.' I angle the phone further away from the sun.

'Adolf Hitler,' I begin. 'Great, thanks Harry.'

'Go on.'

'Fine. Adolf Hitler, Janis Joplin, Syd Barrett, Jim Morrison, Marilyn Monroe, Christina Ricci, Zelda Fitzgerald, Princess Diana, Vincent van Gogh, Susanna Kaysen, Al Pacino, Kurt Cobain–'

'Well?'

'Well what?'

'Okay, forget Hitler, but most of the people on this list are exceptional artists, people who've really contributed something to society.'

'Half of them killed themselves.'

'But don't you see what I'm getting at?'

'It says at the bottom of the page that the list is unconfirmed. These people weren't necessarily diagnosed.'

Harry takes the phone back. 'Look, the point is, who's to say that just because you exhibit certain personality traits you're, I don't know, *mentally ill*? I play all my best roles when I'm in the throes of despair. Maybe you're just an artist, Gretchen.'

I gulp my pint too fast and hide a hiccup.

'The world's most brilliant people exhibit some sort of demonic crazed energy from time to time,' he continues, the happiest he's looked all day. 'And that's when they get things done, because of that intensity. That's what half of society is afraid of, but grateful for at the same time.' Harry gives me the most caring look I've ever seen him give. I imagine it's a look he learnt at LAMDA. 'Hey, you've been through a lot lately. You don't need to define yourself.'

I look up at the sky, at the pure, complete blueness of it, and wonder what I should do with the rest of my life.

'You guys still playing?' asks Jen, cheeks burning with rage.

Every musician in the orchestra had forgotten how to play. The violinists' bows dropped at their sides, the pianist's head lay on the keys. The auditorium was thick with silence.

Harry loses interest in his story and turns to me. 'Hey, what happened to Simon?'

I pick at the table, digging my fingers into the wood, feeling a splinter work its way under my thumbnail. 'We broke up. Didn't work out. I guess I wanted him to have some kind of normalising effect on me.' I push the splinter further in, until it draws blood. 'I've realised I'm okay with not being normal.'

Harry smiles, then bursts into tears. 'I want to go home.'

Jen picks up the dice. 'Well, this was a bad idea.'

'We'll go for sushi,' says Colin. 'Just you and me.'

Jen grins. 'Okay.'

I look at the girl in the maxi dress and wonder whether I should say anything before we leave. I'd like to know her name. But I'm drunk and my hands are shaking, so not today. Today I'll go home. Drink a bit more in the safety of my own home. Send some embarrassing text messages. Write some regrettable tweets. Check my OKCupid account and add a picture of my breasts to my profile.

Colin and Jen give me a hug, and Harry collapses between their shoulders as they walk him home. I walk in the opposite direction.

The Queen's daughter, spoiled as she was, didn't always get what she wanted. Though the Queen bought her robes of the finest silk, trimmed with the softest taffeta, topped with the most sparkling tiaras, what she really wanted and never actually got, was to spend more time with the King. Plus a little serenity in the kingdom. A bit of serenity wouldn't go amiss.

Full of Delirium Tremens, I log in to OKCupid, ready to post a cleavage shot. As I wait for it to load, I open a new window and google 'Artistic Personality'. This is what I find:

Typical traits associated with the *Artistic Personality Type:*

1. Mood swings: *those of the artistic persuasion tend to be quicker to react, and react more strongly than other people.*
2. Creativity: *they tend to be involved in fine arts, music, or literature. They are likely to use a creative approach in all aspects of their lives.*
3. Isolation: *they are liable to spend a great deal of time alone.*
4. Extroversion versus introversion: *artistic types normally alternate between extremes of sociability and social reticence.*
5. Impulsiveness: *they tend to be hedonistic and to make decisions based on impulse rather than as a result of logical and rational thought.*
6. Productivity versus lethargy: *artistic types can be extremely prolific, able to work on large-scale projects for a great deal of time. However, they may also enjoy long and frequent periods of recreation and inactivity.*
7. Sensitivity: *the artistic temperament is likely to be sensitive to the five senses, and more prone to react strongly to these stimuli.*
8. Aggression: *artistic types may get angry more easily than others.*

9. Kindness: *when feeling calm and content, they are likely to be remarkably caring individuals.*

Maybe it's because I'm drunk when I read it. Maybe it's because I'm worried about Harry. Maybe it's because I'm worried nobody's worried about me.

But whatever the reason, when I get to thinking about it, I realise that Harry's right. I don't need to define myself. My sister has been given enough labels her time: psychotic, neurotic, schizophrenic, autistic, depressed, obsessive compulsive, crazy. But it doesn't change a thing as far as I'm concerned. Lottie is still my sister. And I'm still me.

The snow octopus woke up late that morning, with a hangover and a bad case of the horrors.

She felt like all she ever did was get drunk these days. She did it because she was afraid of the dark.

Today, she decided, she was going to take positive action. She was going to buy a torch.

The doctor tells me it sounds like I have Borderline Personality Disorder.

Obviously this comes as no surprise.

He refers me to a community psychiatric nurse for a consultation. Warns me that the clinic tends not to diagnose people with BPD, even if they think they have it, because of the terrible stigma attached. I think that sounds stupid. But I don't get angry. I tell the doctor it's okay, because honestly, the name doesn't matter. I just need some support right now.

Google Maps Saved My Life

He's in there, somewhere. Trapped, like a doll in a doll's house.

Each time I switch on the computer, I create a new fantasy for him.

One day, I like to imagine he's listening to *The Archers*, while cutting his nails over the bin. Another, he might be harvesting virtual crops in a game of Farmville. Another, and my mum's telling him off for putting an empty whisky bottle back in the cupboard. Another still, and he's teaching my sister to say 'turtle' in German, while she sits doing cross-stitch at his feet. Most often of all, I like to imagine that he's working on a long stretch of complex programming code, with two cups of lukewarm coffee beside him, and *Desert Island Discs* playing softly in the background.

But on this particular day, when I switch on the computer, I decide to play out something entirely new.

You know those dreams where you can just click your fingers and time stands still? Where everything in the world freezes, except you?

And you can weave
                    in and out of it all

unnoticed

for as long as you like

until you click your fingers–

and time carries on again, just as before?

You'll have seen it on TV and in films. An early example occurs in The Twilight Zone, back in 1961, in an episode called 'A Kind of Stopwatch'. The protagonist, McNulty, owns a watch that can stop time. More recently, it happened in that Tim Burton movie, *Big Fish*, at the moment where Ewan McGregor's character spots the love of his life.

And you may have seen it in books too. There's the H. G. Wells story 'The New Accelerator', for instance, about a drug that causes you to move so fast that everyone else seems still.

Well, I've witnessed this freezing-time effect first-hand.

The first time I visited, it was out of homesickness. More than homesickness, I guess. Grief. Which is a type of sickness too.

I opened Google, typed in the postcode, and looked at the map. I zoomed in once, then again, until finally I could see it: Ivy Cottage. It had been my family home for twenty-four years, and I knew every stain on the brickwork.

It was a bright day. Most of the trees had leaves on, and the sun was high in the sky. The wheelbarrow rested against the side of the house, and there was washing on the line, curled at the edges in the breeze. It looked like a lovely spring afternoon.

I turned down the lane to get a better view of the front garden. The first thing I saw was the milk by the gate, not yet taken inside. Then I spotted the old sun-lounger. Just the skeleton, no mattress, on the front lawn.

This told me something very important.

Dad hadn't died yet.

Whatever moment in time this set of pictures was taken, the disease hadn't yet spread to my father's spine. I knew this because, as soon as it did, the first thing he did was move the sun-lounger to the patio at the back of the house. He'd use his Zimmer frame to get from his bed to the back door, and he'd sit on the lounger to get some fresh air.

I began to look for other clues. The windows were all dark, but I zoomed in on each one, just to make sure. The first two contained nothing. But when I closed in on the third one, at the top-right of the house, I saw the outline of a jewellery box.

At the point that this picture was taken, then, Lottie was still living at home. Which was over three years ago. Which meant my sister hadn't yet moved in with Rob, which meant she hadn't yet become engaged, which meant she hadn't yet tried to slit her wrists in the bath.

I moved further down the lane and looked onto the driveway. One silver car; one red. So at the very moment this picture was taken, Mum and Dad were both at home.

'Hello!' I called. 'Mum! Dad! Lottie! Are you there?'

I wanted to shake my computer until they fell out.

Naturally there are limits to the zoom function on Google

Maps. But the longer I stared at my house, from every angle I could get at it, the more easily I began to imagine myself opening a door and stepping inside. As if I was really there, and the house was really there, but it was just time that had stood still.

I tried to picture each member of my family; what room they might be in, what they might be doing at the exact moment the photo had been taken.

Mum was probably in the lounge, lying on the sofa in front of *Murder She Wrote*. Or, since it was lunchtime, maybe she was in the kitchen making parsnip soup, paused in a freeze-frame just as the wooden spoon had reached her mouth. I could almost taste it.

Lottie would most likely be in her room. She usually hid there, doing craft on the carpet. I could see her now, halfway through stuffing a felt frog, with a strange, sad darkness in her eyes.

And Dad? Well, Dad was in his office. No question. If only the camera had been able to travel around to the back of the house, I'd see him sitting at the computer by the window, his fingers midway through pushing down the letters 'a' and 'n' on the keyboard. Yeah, Dad was in there alright.

My whole family was inside this magical puzzle.

It became a sort of habit, I guess. An addiction. I went back to look at the house every day, imagining what everyone was doing. Remembering.

The mothball smell in the porch. The Wellington boots by the back door. The crumbs in the bread bin. The poppies on the bathroom tiles. The light bulb that never got replaced on the stairs.

This place where my dad wasn't about to die.

Where he and my mum weren't afraid to sit within the same four walls as one another. Where my sister hadn't been committed to psychiatric hospital, and where everyone was doing okay, and nothing truly bad had ever happened to us.

One day, when I zoom in on the sun-lounger in the front garden, I allow myself to play out a new fantasy.

What if today, I think, Dad is doing something different?

Today, he is writing me a letter. On his screen it says something like this:

My darling daughter,
    This is the hardest letter I have ever had to write. But before I die, I need to tell you how much you mean to me. Ever since the day you were b

And at this exact moment in time, the exact moment that Google once chose to drive their camera-topped car through a hamlet in Buckinghamshire, my dad had been frozen mid-sentence, writing a message just for me.

I stand in the doorway, watching, willing him to come back to life and finish the letter.

But I know that's impossible.

Even if he was to come back to life, he wouldn't finish it. He'd sigh, wipe away his tears, and he'd press backspace until it ate up every word on his screen. Then he'd go back to that long, complex code, because it was so much easier, so much less painful.

I tiptoe away.

You know, in just about every example, in those books and films where time stands still, there are always repercussions. In 'The New Accelerator', the drug causes your heart to beat so fast that you could die at any minute. In *Big Fish*, after time has stood still, it 'moves extra fast to catch up'. And in The Twilight Zone, perhaps most frightening of all, McNulty's special stopwatch breaks, and time remains frozen for eternity.

I look again at that empty sun-lounger in the front garden, then I zoom out. From the dark, yellow vein of the A-road running alongside the house, I zoom out again. And again. Until I am staring at the Earth from space.

I think about particles and waves and movement and energy, and all the things my dad used to teach me about when I was a little girl. If everything in the universe were to pause, I think, there would be no light.

So I take a deep breath and switch off my computer–

and time carries on, just as before.

Possible Subject For A Future Novel

'I read your book,' Steve calls from the bathroom. There's a lull, filled only by the steady stream of pee.

His flat is smaller than I was expecting it to be. Open plan, with the kitchen and living room joined together.

'First story was terrible,' he continues. 'Childish pap.'

I try to grow used to the sight of things. A peace lily, dropping its leaves into the sink; goose feather on the mantelpiece; Orla Kiely tea towel, hanging on the oven door. Traces of this woman I'll never know.

I look inside cupboards and think about Steve's pee. How hot it is as it comes out. If there's any steam in the seconds before it hits the bowl.

'Tell you what,' he calls. 'Let's watch some telly.'

It's the first time he's invited me here. Normally we meet in Pret a Manger. Once we went to a hotel room. We've never had sex. It's not what we do.

'Okay,' I say quietly, too quietly for him to hear through the bathroom wall, and I go to the French windows and stand on the balcony.

It's March, and a cold March at that. There's a drainpipe on the corner of the building opposite, and I wonder if I can jump far enough to grab it, climb down four storeys and run away into the night.

'There you are.' Steve's arm coils around my waist, and I smell garlic on his breath. 'The view's better in spring.

See that tree over there?' He points to a small, sad sapling in the middle of the road. 'That'll grow cherries. Ever picked cherries?'

Looking at the tree makes my kidneys hurt. Makes me think of hospitals. The tree has a cage around its trunk, and the tarmac splits either side of it. Did someone plant it after the tarmac had split? Surely one tiny tree can't have roots big enough to split open a road.

'You know, in Japan, they watch the cherry blossom spread northward, from Okinawa up to Tokyo. Takes three months. South to north. South to north, baby.' He's doing it again. That trick. First an insult, then a thrill. I think of his wife. Imagine how she feels as she sips her lapsang souchong on spring mornings, wondering how long the blossom will last before it falls onto the Manchester streets and turns to mush.

'So many sleazeballs are gonna want to get in your pants if you get that thing published,' he whispers. 'It's one filthy fucking book.' His fingers trail up my thigh, nudging my hemline. 'You'll get what you deserve. You'll get it, girl.'

'Maybe I don't want it,' I say, shivering. 'Let's go in.'

I was in the middle of a smoked salmon sandwich when we first met. It was eleven o'clock in the morning – too early to be eating lunch – but that didn't matter, because he was already drunk.

'Load of fucking rubbish,' he slurred, pushing his copy of the Metro across the table so it rested in the empty place between us. 'Bad news *this*. Shit news *that*. Everything's fucking fucked.'

I put down my book, a raunchy Henry Miller, and,

feeling nihilistic, smiled.

'Steve,' he said, smoothing out his suit jacket with tremorous hands. 'Bit hungover.'

I nodded and finished my sandwich, watching the pigeons strut around Piccadilly Gardens. I could sense Steve watching me. He grimaced as I dropped crumbs onto the tabletop.

'Bet you're a cappuccino type,' he said finally, pointing at my cup. 'Plain old black coffee guy, me. No cappuccino and no fucking *novels*.' He pointed at my reading matter.

That morning, I'd been to an art gallery to see an exhibition on radical feminist art, I'd taken a stroll along the canal, and I'd stopped at Pret a Manger for some smoked salmon and Henry Miller. He was right. What a load of pretentious wank.

'What's your story, then?' he asked. 'Why the face like a smacked arse?'

I smiled again. This is what my life had come to. The drunk guy with vomit stains on his lapel was asking me what was the matter.

'Let me guess,' he said, not giving me time to answer. 'Beneath the veneer of cosy middle-class existence there lurks some terrible secret? What could it be... Daddy issues? Looking for love in all the wrong places? I don't know... struggling to finish your doctorate?'

His words stung. For a moment, I enjoyed the pain. I took a breath, then said: 'That was the old Gretchen. The new one is just struggling to finish her day.'

'Who's Gretel?' Steve asked.

'Gretchen,' I sighed. 'I'm talking about myself in the third person.'

'Third person,' Steve laughed. 'Right.' He almost

seemed like a nice guy when he laughed. I wondered what he did for a living. Something in an office, maybe. Solicitor. No. Salesman.

'What about you?' I asked. 'What's your story?'

'My wife's a bitch,' he said, then crumpled a little. The noise of the coffee machine meant he had to shout to be heard: 'But I can't leave her!'

'Why not?' I called back.

Steve rolled his eyes. 'Ever been cheated on?' he yelled.

I thought about Leon and my mum. It probably never happened, but it made me feel sick to think about it. I thought about all the times I'd cheated on people. I felt guilty, but not sick. I shook my head.

The coffee machine stopped grinding beans, and Steve said quietly: 'I need to find a way to make it even.'

'How?'

He looked at the book in front of me, noticing its erotic cover for the first time. 'I bet you're into that *Fifty Shades* shit,' he said with a grin, then leaned across the table. 'I bet you like to be treated *mean*.'

I lifted my cup to my lips. This is the problem with being a writer. I should have walked away, but I was too busy alchemising the moment into words on a page. 'What makes you say that?' I asked.

Steve breathed stale whisky into my nostrils. 'Just a hunch, Miss Cappuccino.'

I put down the cup on my book cover, obscuring the naked woman's breasts. 'Tell me about your wife's affair,' I said.

He began to talk, and I listened, just as I listened every time we met from then on.

I never told him at any of our meetings that I was

drinking plain old black coffee.

Steve pours us both a Kahlua. 'The only booze she won't notice is missing. Lefover from Christmas. Tastes of baby puke,' he says, handing me a large glass. 'Drink up.'

I sit on the sofa and drink, keeping my knees two inches apart. He told me he liked that the second time we met. This is the eleventh. I remember details.

He switches on the TV and the sound slices between us. *Man Versus Food.* A show about the most repulsive man on earth. Every episode, he eats a depressingly similar mound of bread, meat, cheese, and sauce, always in a race against the clock. Tonight, the audience cheers as he attempts the world's biggest BLT. Steve and I sit side by side, staring at a bun oozing mustard mayonnaise.

Eventually he turns to me. 'You need to use the third person,' he tells me, 'in your book. Otherwise everyone will think it's about you.'

'Steve,' I say, looking at the fat man on TV, 'it *is* about me.'

He takes the controller and hits the red button. Our reflections appear on the screen. It strikes me, for the first time, that Steve looks a lot older than forty-eight. I wonder if he lied about his age. *I* did. Told him I'm twenty-one. Every new encounter is a chance for reinvention.

There's a hand-embroidered cushion on the wicker chair in the corner. I wonder if it was a gift. Try to imagine Steve's wife's face as she opened the wrapping paper, held the fabric to her chest. 'I don't even know her name,' I say suddenly. 'And I'm in her home.'

'Drink your Kahlua,' he says. 'You need to be out in an hour.'

Steve is getting aroused. I can tell. It happened in the hotel room, where we drank gin from the minibar and talked about what a fuck-up she is. Janine. I'm going to call her that. Suits her.

I want to tell him I should go, that this is no way for him to get over the affair, that this sad attempt at sadomasochism really isn't doing it for me any more. But he slams his glass on the coffee table and grabs me, making me spill Kahlua onto my tights. 'Women,' he groans, pinching my back. I think he's trying to cuddle me. 'Women are shit.' It sounds like he's crying. 'I love her, Gretel. What am I going to do?'

After four and a half minutes – I watch the clock on the mantelpiece, next to the goose feather – he stops. Drains his drink. Like a ten-year-old boy, sucking up his chocolate milk before bed, ending with a burp.

'Are you ready?' he asks, staring at my chest.

I put my knees firmly together and ask if it's okay if we put *Man Versus Food* back on for a bit, but he says no. He takes me by the hand and leads me to the bedroom. Kneeling, he rummages around in what's obviously not his side of the wardrobe.

The bedroom is cosy. Matching pine furniture. Proper stuff; not IKEA. Expensive. A collection of Audrey Hepburn postcards are blue-tacked on the wall by the window. A red silk scarf is draped over the dressing table mirror. There's a pile of biographies beside the bed. I like this woman. Steve's right; I have a lot in common with her.

Finally, he stops rummaging. 'Wear this,' he says, handing me a pink nightie. Or at least, it *was* pink. It's faded, pinky-grey, like the inside of a seashell. The label reads 'St. Michael, size 10'. It's Marks and Spencer before it was Marks and Spencer; that makes it over a decade old.

'Wear it and get into bed.'

'Steve. You know we've agreed we won't. That's not what this is about.'

He looks at me in disgust. It's the look that got me talking to him in the first place. 'Okay,' I mumble. 'I'm going to the bathroom.'

'It's at the end of the hall.'

'I know. I heard you pee.'

He's left the toilet seat up and hasn't bothered to flush. His piss is very yellow for this time of night. He must be dehydrated.

I take off my cardigan, vest, skirt, tights, letting them fall into a heap. Then I put on the nightie, which smells of mothballs. She hasn't worn it for a long time. Maybe she's bigger than a ten these days. I'm a twelve. It drags across my chest, pulls across the middle, forming an unsightly horizontal dip in the fabric.

I splash my face with water. Remove my hairband. Let my hair fall, full of kinks, down to my shoulders. Look at myself in the mirror. The wrinkles, worse than a thirty-year-old's wrinkles should be. Dark circles, spots from too many nights out, a wild stare in the eyes. I open the medicine cabinet. Lancôme. Clinique. Neal's Yard. It's aspirational stuff. The way mine would be if I earned at least £5 an hour more than I do. And if I really cared.

I pretend to be Janine as I run my fingers over the bottles. I've had a hard day at work, the balls of my feet are killing me, my husband's a dick, I've got dry skin. I settle on the Clinique, and rub great dollops of it over my neck, my shoulders, the insides of my thighs. Imagine I'm a big slab of meat. It's *Man Versus Food* and I'm slathering myself in mustard mayonnaise. Except I don't smell of mayonnaise; I smell of – I don't know – lavender, sea urchins, whatever. As I spread cream over my thighs, I remind myself that sex isn't part of the deal.

'Bet you want to crawl around on the floor, don't you?' asked Steve, loosening his tie and pouring us gins from the minibar. 'Lick the dirt off my shoes and shit.'

'I don't know,' I said. 'I'll settle for a gin,'

'How many hotel rooms have you been to with strangers, then? Fifty? A hundred?' He sat on the bed next to me.

'A few,' I said, enjoying the newness of being in a hotel with Steve, but hoping he wasn't going to get carried away. The first few times we met I'd enjoyed the buzz of being insulted. Steve said the things I'd always felt about myself, and it was a relief to finally hear them said out loud. Over the weeks though, I'd grown more unsure. I didn't see how adpoting these roles was helping either of us. Besides, Steve's wife was no more of a whore than I was. Maybe it would have been nice to be called a hero for a change. Or at the very least, a human.

'Steve,' I said, brushing his hand with mine. 'I'd like you to read my book.'

He opened his mouth. I may as well have just told him I was an alien.

'It's only a first draft. It's not done yet.'

'Why me?' he asked. 'I hate reading.'

'Because I know you'll be honest,' I said, which was a lie. Actually, it was because I wanted him to understand me. I knew it was a long shot.

He stood up and paced around the room, touching the

wipe-clean curtains, fiddling with the electric cord on the kettle, picking up the Bible and then throwing it onto the armchair. 'Okay,' he said eventually. 'I'll read your book if you do something for me.'

I looked at the fire escape intructions on the back of the door. 'What?'

'I want you to come to my house. See where the bitch sleeps. I want to call *you* a bitch in my house. Maybe in my bed. It will help me. Honestly.'

I closed my eyes. Wondered what Steve would make of my writing. Whether any of it would surprise him. If it'd turn him on. If he'd feel any remorse. 'Alright,' I said, sliding back on the sheets.

Steve sat on the bed again, this time nestled closer to me, and he talked about 'the bitch'. Sometimes my mind wandered, and I forgot whether he was talking about me, or his wife, or all of womankind.

I'm gazing into the toilet bowl as if it holds the future. I sit on the floor and take a good look. Two grey hairs float in the pee. I get an urge to stick my finger in, but I can hear Steve stomping around in the other room.

Leaving my clothes on the floor, I head into the bedroom, and find Steve standing on what looks like her side of the bed, completely naked.

'Get in,' he says, motioning at the sheets. I've never seen him without his clothes before. It's not attractive. I climb into bed. He looks at me for a few moments. 'Your tits are too big. Your tits are wrong.'

I pull the covers over myself, feeling the blush spread up to my neck.

'You're a whore, Margaret.'

Margaret is *her*: Janine. 'Don't hit me,' I say, which sounds ridiculous, because he's never hit me, and maybe I'd quite like to be hit, once, just gently, just until the emptiness disappears.

'Tell me you're sorry,' he says.

'I'm sorry.'

'Tell me you won't do it again.'

'I won't do it again.' This is more familiar; this is the script we're supposed to follow.

'Bitch,' he blurts. 'You bloody bitch, Margaret.' Steve is getting hard. I can hear it in his voice before I can see it.

'I'll never cheat again,' I say unconvincingly. 'I promise.'

His erection is putting me off. It's revolting.

'Steve,' I say, suddenly thinking back to the day we met, when he had vomit on his lapel. 'Has your opinion of me changed since you read my book?'

Steve looks straight through me. 'Tell me you're a good girl,' he says, stroking himself. 'Tell me you're a wise old woman.'

I tell him I'm getting tired of this whole charade.

'Tell me you're a princess.' he groans. 'Tell me you're a supermodel. Tell me you're my mummy.'

I tell him I have to go.

He collapses on the mattress, crying again. This time he doesn't even try to hide it. 'Please don't write about this in your fucking book, Gretel,' he whimpers.

'Brutality and weakness are so often the same thing,' I say gently, as if that's some kind of answer, and I walk out. I go back to the bathroom and put on my clothes, then I piss, right on top of his piss, and flush.

'Goodbye, Steve,' I call.

'Bye bye, Miss Cappuccino,' he sobs, and I close the door.

At the top of the stairs, I pass a woman. She has short black hair and a frown. Can't tell if she's got dry skin. I brush the sleeve of her coat with mine. She doesn't notice.

For the first time, I wonder what on earth Janine sees in him. Maybe she's stupid. Maybe she's sad. Maybe she's afraid. It's not my life, I guess. I don't have to understand.

I stop thinking about her life, and I think about my own. Not everything I do has to be a possible subject for a future novel. I don't have to fall in love with nasty acts because they make great sentences.

I can be the hero of my own story. But I can also switch to the third person.

Out in the street, I listen to my shoes on the tarmac as I head for the city centre, and I watch the road in front of me split open.

Limited Dreamers

It's one of the phrases they'd learnt at the Council. Somebody else's idea of somebody else.

Busy mums, who buy Burger King and dress their daughters as princesses. Who watch *Who Wants to be a Millionaire?* – once the kids are finally bloody asleep – shouting answers at the telly like maybe if they're loud enough, the £32,000 will be theirs. Who take an all-inclusive-one-week holiday to Marbella each July, and come back saying 'Next year we'll try Greece'. But they never do.

These people are Limited Dreamers, and they do not exist.

The girls had worked at the Council for a very short time, brought in via a temping agency, dismissed at a week's notice.

Both girls had unusual names. One was a kind of fruit. The other was German; it caught on your tongue like a mouthful of lace. On the second day of their unemployment, they sat in a bar. They had arranged to meet to talk about signing on, working tax credits, housing benefits: things which scared them both. But as soon as they saw one another, all that stuff flew out of their heads.

Instead, they swapped books and drank coffee and

drew strange pictures in felt-tips, as they talked about dragons and kissing and the pros and cons of moving to Seattle. They talked about tarot cards and film-making and just how perfect you could expect someone's teeth to be at thirty-five. They talked about their own friends, and the friends they wanted to become to each other.

It was only the third time they had spoken. The first was in the staff canteen, where they'd discussed the possibility of selling their bodies for cash, or maybe just their knickers or socks, but only if it counted as Feminist, and only if it was in the name of Art.

The second time they'd met was at a literary event, where American cult writer Tao Lin was headlining. All the writers at the event used present tense and brand names. They all acted like everything was empty, and sometimes that emptiness was funny, but sometimes it was worse than sad, it was just nothing.

The girls had half hated the event. They sat at the back of the room, sighing, and one of them accidentally kicked Tao Lin's bum, because he was sitting in front of them.

But they had half loved the event too, and loving it made them horny and uncomfortable.

Today, they were glad they had felt-tips. There was no guilt in stationery. Stationery was pre– words. It was pre–love letters and terrible drawings of your own hand. It was pre– let's-write-our-initials-on-our-books-and-CDs, and pre– I've-underlined-every-number-on-this-phone-bill-that-I-have-a-problem-with. It was pre– why-I'm-breaking-up-with-you-notes and pre– bullet-point-lists-of-everything-you-ever-did-to-hurt-me.

It seemed like everyone thought everyone else was autistic lately.

So the girls talked about friendship, and they talked about this 'Manic Pixie Dream Girl' article they had read. In the article, the author argues that men fall in love with women who remind them of Zooey Deschanel, women who bake cupcakes and dance in the rain and ride bicycles with baskets on, and wear peephole bras and have spitting competitions. Men fall in love with women like this because they fall in love with an ideal, a character in a book or a film, not a real life human-woman who has still has that ruddy verruca, the one she hasn't been able to shift for seven years, who breaks wind every time she is about to fall asleep, who keeps a list of everyone she's ever fucked and how terrible it was, and who once slapped someone in the face three times just for saying hello.

The girls talked about avocados and pineapples and exactly what shade of blue they like the best, and whether it would be called teal or cyan, and what the difference was between teal and cyan. They talked about Kate Zambreno and Sheila Heti and Miranda July, and how exciting it was that Sheila Heti and Miranda July were friends, and how amazing it would be to be friends with Sheila Heti and Miranda July. Or Kate Zambreno. They talked about polyamory. And they talked about everything, *everything*, but signing on, working tax credits, housing benefits, or how they were going to function in the real world after today was over.

The girl with the name like fruit – let's call her Banana – she coloured in a zine she was making: bright orange felt-tip bubbles next to a collage of a woman's torso.

The other girl, the one with the German name – let's call her Schmidt – she was quieter. The inside of her head did figures of eight. This was her second day on antidepressants, and figures of eight were better than the shapes she was making before. She was drawing a brainstorm in purple pen, and the brainstorm was entitled *What I Want From Life*. She had only got as far as 'a dressing gown', and was now feeling the roof of her mouth with her finger, wondering what her friend looked like naked.

'The best thing about this,' said Banana, colouring so hard she was making a hole in the page, 'is that we've got all the time in the world. No limits.'

Schmidt thought about how long two decades might feel, and the fact that once she hit fifty she'd be as good as dead. She wondered what she was going to fill the rest of her life with. It felt like she'd already got to wherever she was heading, and she couldn't think of anything she wanted to happen next, except for that damn dressing gown.

But still she nodded, and as she did so, she remembered the day at Brownies two decades ago – so *that's* how long two decades feels – when the old ladies brought their tarnished silver, and some of it was so old you couldn't do anything with it, there was just no way to make it shine.

Three hours after they arrived, they left.

Schmidt had a doctor's appointment, and now that the girls had talked about being friends, it seemed appropriate that they go to the appointment together. They walked to the surgery, and sat in the waiting room, and Schmidt told her friend about her sister. She told her that her sister had been sectioned seven weeks ago, and the words came out all wrong, and then she went in to see the doctor.

When they left the surgery, Schmidt's sister walked beside them in a straitjacket, kicking stones and threatening suicide.

Had it been too soon to bring up the sectioned sister? Banana had a tattoo of a ghost on her elbow. Schmidt hoped that would make it okay.

Eventually Schmidt's sister began to lag behind, until she couldn't keep up, and the girls found somewhere new, another bar, with a table out on the street, just right for felt-tips, and there was a sign that said 'fresh lemonade'.

They sat beside an abandoned scooter and a toy gun. Schmidt put out her arms, and wondered if her freckles were appearing in the sunshine. Banana joked about the rubbish skip behind her, said that it suited her, that she looked like Stig of the Dump, and they laughed.

'Sorry,' said a waitress, a girl of about their age, with a pierced lip and a look about her that said that in another life, under different circumstances, they might have been friends. 'Customers aren't allowed out here after 5 p.m. Would you like to sit inside?'

Banana, eyes on the toy gun, said: 'We'll go elsewhere.'

The waitress walked away. She didn't have any tattoos on her arms, no trailing ghosts. There was silence.

'I think I'll head home,' said Banana. 'My husband will be wondering where I am.'

Schmidt's mind did a panicky figure of eight.

They walked towards the tram stop, talking about Banana's husband, and what he did for a living, and how strange it was that their job at the Council was over. They agreed that the next time they met they would discuss signing on, working tax credits, and housing benefits. They reassured each other that *something would come up*, that *it always does*, that there was *plenty of time*.

Outside Morrisons, at the back of the tram stop, Banana said that she thought she was getting a whitehead on her nose. Schmidt said she was glad that she had moved to Manchester, that she didn't miss Glasgow as much as she used to, and that she thought she might buy a crate of beer for tea.

They hugged and kissed the air next to each other's left ears. The air, where it had been kissed, didn't fizzle or pop. It just went on being air, the same old air they had always known, and they weren't manic pixie dream girls, and there were limits to everything, including themselves, and they said goodbye.

How To Be An Alcoholic Writer

A Twelve-Step Programme

1. Set small goals for yourself.

Let's get this straight. Becoming an alcoholic writer isn't going to happen for you overnight. It takes a serious commitment, and a willingness to devote thousands of hours, and pounds, to the activity.

My name's Gretchen. And I am an alcoholic writer.

Achieving this took a lot of practice. There was that first drink, on the sofa with my dad when I was a baby. According to my parents, my first word was 'beer'. My second was 'more'. Then at the dinner table, aged seven, it was half a glass of wine to go with my Sunday roast. Aged twelve it was gin, poured into a Tizer bottle, sipped in the loos before Double Maths. Aged fifteen: Southern Comfort, quaffed round the back of WHSmith's. Seventeen and alone, so alone, glugging White Lightning and writing poems that rip off Sylvia Plath.

2. Study the drinking habits of alcoholic writers you admire.

Each writer has their own unique drinking style. When you're starting out, it pays to study the greats.

There's Hemingway, who supposedly said 'write drunk; edit sober'. His liver stuck right out of his belly. Dorothy Parker, who drank her scotch in continuous sips, so she was rarely drunk, but seldom sober. Raymond Chandler, who compared alcohol to love: magic, intimate and routine. He wrote the ending to *The Blue Dahlia* on a strict diet of alcohol and glucose injections. John Berryman, who started writing a novel about recovery, but gave up to throw himself off a bridge. Raymond Carver, who quit booze and couldn't write for a year - played bingo and ate doughnuts instead. Stephen King, whose family staged an intervention. And Dylan Thomas, who once claimed to have put away eighteen straight whiskies. Five days later, he died.

3. To be a good drinker, drink every day.

It's no good trying a tipple once or twice, and then deciding you prefer hanging out at the shopping centre, hitting a tennis ball against a wall, or practising for your Grade Four piano exam. If you want to become an alcoholic writer, you're going to have to work at getting the right attitude from the start.

Wearing glasses helps. So does having freckles you hate or a fear of eating in public or hair that's the wrong shade of brown. Whatever it is that makes you feel that little bit different, that little bit more likely to tell people your favourite novel is 'a toss up between *The Catcher in the Rye* and *The Outsider*'. That leads to you sitting by the air vent outside the staff canteen, penning haiku about being buried alive, drinking vodka masquerading as water, while your workmates chat about Brad Pitt and Slim Fast.

That life is not for you. Keep writing those haiku, and after each 5/7/5, don't forget to take a big old swig. The sort of swig that makes your stomach lining burn, and that screaming in your skull into more of a grim whisper.

4. Try 'morning drinking'.

In the morning, you're at your least self-critical, so that's an ideal time to reach for the box of wine under your bed. Take the box into the shower with you. Don't know what happened last night? Never mind. At least you've got the box.

5. Try 'spontaneous drinking'.

It's important to get into some sort of rhythm with your boozing. For example, you could drink for two hours in the morning, take a leisurely walk to the offie, drink for three hours in the afternoon, zigzag to the offie, drink for five hours in the evening, careen to the offie, try to write some of your book, then pass out. Every so often, though, you might want to shake things up a bit. Get yourself out of your comfort zone and force yourself to drink even when you're not in the mood. This may yield interesting results. (Don't worry, you can wear long sleeves all summer.)

6. Drink what you know.

This one's been terribly overused, but it bears repeating: *drink what you know*. Grab a Fairtrade Merlot every day on the way home from work. It's not the cheapest bottle – it's £5.49 – so they'll never suspect you have a drinking problem.

- It's clearly to go with your dinner.

- It's for you and your imaginary lover.
- It's for the stressful day you've had (again).
- It's the last time you'll ever do this, and then you'll clean up, honest.
- Just one more bottle (and a few cans of Stella) until you've got this damn story finished.
- It'll help get the creative juices going.
- It'll stop you self-censoring.
- It's medicinal.
- It's Fairtrade.
- It's basically saving the world.

7. The essence of drinking is redrinking.

Think you've had enough? Of course not. Drink some more. Drink until you're sitting at the back of the bar, spilling real ale down your pyjama top, writing spidery sentences onto that (probably unimportant) letter from the bank.

Feel the genius flow from your pen point.

According to Stephen Hawking it means that if she goes into space by the time she gets back to earth her buddleia plant will have a better chance of replanting than she will. Her beautiful purple buddleia will be like heavy plants from the future... ANYWAY, we all know about you and your LOVE OF BUDDLEIA. We know you don't give a shit about the stuff. We know you've had every chance to tell us how much you CARE about every FUCKING BUTTERFLY that's ever landed on this STUPID SHITTING PLANT.

It's the best thing you've ever written. It's– closing time.

That doorstep looks comfy. It's freezing out here. There's a man in a shellsuit coming towards you.

8. Drink as if you're drinking to deadline.

Being under pressure helps. Losing your home, losing your dad, getting fired, being in a fire, failing friendships, failing your PhD, getting diagnosed with Borderline Personality Disorder, not getting diagnosed with something 'better', your sister taking an overdose, your mum having a nervous breakdown, more letters from the bank. All these things will give you plenty to write about, and plenty to drink about. But remember, even when you're feeling delicate, you're still going to have to...

9. Learn to deal with rejection.

It happens to us all. And the more you drink – the more publicly – the more likely it is you're going to experience rejection at some point in your career. The good news is that this will only make you drink more, and drink harder. A bad blog review, for example, might lead to a three-day bender. A bad review in the national press might lead to a stomach pump. I've never been reviewed in the national press, so I wouldn't know. Sometimes, not being reviewed in the national press will also lead to a stomach pump.

10. Avoid clichés.

Avoid them like the plague.

Each alcoholic writer's path is a highly individual

journey. You are a unique snowflake, crying over spilt cider and unpaid electricity bills. Your last story didn't make sense and you told all your Twitter followers you want to die. Roll with the punches. Salvation only costs another £5.49. *It's Fairtrade.*

11. Beware of losing the plot.

My name's Gretchen. And I'm an alcoholic writer.

Recently, I did lose the plot. I went to see my doctor, told her I couldn't get any writing done. She asked how long I'd felt this way. What time of day did I feel worst? Did I have any friends? How much did I drink?

She left the room for a moment, and came back with a woman with red hair. 'I'm Debbie,' the woman said. 'I'm on the Community Alcohol Team.'

Debbie and I worked through a list. More questions.

First drink?
Can't remember.
Can't remember?
I've always drunk.
Always?
My first word was beer.
Really, Gretchen?
Yes, Debbie. Seriously.
[Debbie writes something down.] **How much are you drinking?**
I don't know. Too much.
Do you think you can stop?
[Tears.] *No. Please don't make me stop.*

I was given an alcohol self-help guide. It had pictures of drinks in it. The drinks had faces. Some of them were smiling. Some of them were not smiling. They were all absolute tossers.

Debbie got me to fill in a drink diary, so we could 'assess how bad the situation is'. The recommended maximum for a woman is fourteen units a week. The following week I tried to cut down. I had sixty-seven-point-three.

Filling in that diary was the first bit of writing I'd done in weeks.

Since then, I've not had any alcohol. I've been sober for forty-three days. I'm currently addicted to milkshake and cashew nuts and diet coke and incense and jumping up and down and cheese. And getting new tattoos. I'm still overdrawn.

Every two weeks, I go to a clinic. Sometimes I visit a treatment unit and attend support meetings. I take six tablets a day to help reduce cravings. The tablets give me diarrhoea. But they do work. A bit.

12. Learn the rules... and then break them.

The beauty of becoming an alcoholic writer is that you don't have to keep drinking to retain your status. Once an alcoholic writer, always an alcoholic writer. Unless you stop writing.

But even though many writers haven't touched a drop of booze in years, that doesn't make teetotalism easy. There are withdrawal symptoms for a start, and the responses other writers have when you tell them you've quit.

You might lose friends. Grow anxious, feel trapped inside your own head, hate going out, loathe staying in, detest the person you've become. When you talk to your peers, you might sound like you're giving a lecture. Like there really is some kind of 'twelve-step programme' to getting where you've got, and you're somehow qualified to tell everyone else how it's done.

But if you *are* an alcoholic writer, and you *do* manage to quit drinking, you never know, you might, just might, start to mend, and write – and get *really* bad diarrhoea – and live to tell the tale.

And if it all goes wrong for you, and you find yourself relapsing, fucking up your liver, losing your flat, your friends, your sanity, then remember what your old director used to tell you when you stumbled over your lines in that Sarah Kane play. Cancel and continue. That's all there is to it. Just cancel and continue.

Any Other Mouth

This mouth is like any other mouth. It whispers sweet nothings, tells terrible lies, snogs people it doesn't fancy when it's drunk on a Saturday night. This mouth is pissed when it says its marriage vows. It breathes whisky, stutters and stumbles, cracks as it makes promises it knows it can't keep. This mouth belongs to my father. It says the word 'love' on its wedding day. And despite everything, it really does mean it.

This mouth is like any other mouth. It sings lullabies and it screams. It has a scar running down its top lip, but only recently has it learnt true pain. It sings along to Dire Straits in a voice that splinters with agony. It snogs people it doesn't fancy when it's drunk on a Saturday night. It is a mouth that is bent on revenge. This mouth belongs to my mother. 'I haven't done anything wrong,' it tells me, on the phone at a motorway service station. 'Don't tell your father.'

This mouth, too, is like any other mouth. It laughs and it gets covered in tears. It calls people 'evil' and it says 'Did you hear that? What about that? You think I'm making it up, don't you? Am I going mad?' It speaks like a child to hide its anger. It says some of the most beautiful things I have ever heard. This mouth, the mouth that looks most in the world like my own, my sister's mouth is saying 'die'.

This mouth, even this one, which belongs to me, is like

any other mouth. It burps and recites poetry. It swears in front of children, and it overuses intensifiers even though it recognises how pointless they are. It says things like *literally awful* and *totally unfair* and *so wrong*. Over the years, it has sported five braces, including a head brace, and it has never quite recovered. It kisses far more mouths good night than it does good morning. It says 'I'm sorry', over and over and over. It says 'never again'. It says 'oops'. It says 'sorry'. Oops. Sorry.

You know the drill: this mouth is no different to the others. This mouth belongs to the big brother I never had. It gives me the advice that only a big brother can give. It says things like, 'Don't worry, it doesn't make you a bad person.' And, 'Guess who's coming to surprise you this weekend?' And, 'Let's drive to the hills; you look like you could do with a break.' Now and then, in the evenings, after three glasses of wine, this mouth says things like 'I read your book. Dad would've been impressed. I'm so proud.' When I prepare to go away, to escape somewhere, as occasionally I do, it says, 'Look after yourself, little sis. I'll see you on the other side.'

Actually, if you listen hard enough, that's what all mouths are saying. See you on the other side. See you on the other side.

Like You

If you've got the right soundtrack, walking home in the rain isn't so bad. Even if it's November, and you've had a dull day at work, and you're hungry, tired and cold. Even if your left shoe has a hole in it and is starting to squelch. In fact, it is under this exact set of circumstances that you are most likely to realise how glad you are to be alive.

Go on: turn the music up a little.

As you walk past the pub on the corner, smell the chips, scampi, vinegar and stale beer. Look at the drunks huddling outside for a quick fag. Allow yourself a gulp of smoky air and be surprised by how much you enjoy it.

Take a short-cut through the university. Imagine you're an academic, with a long, stripy scarf and an outmoded hairstyle. Be relieved that this is no longer you. Note the darkening sky ahead; the clouds are almost purple. When you pass the English Literature department, think back to this time last year. Remember how terrible you felt. Like you had reached the end of everything. Like you could no longer walk because you had forgotten how to move.

But look at you now. Seriously: look. There are your hands, hanging at your sides. Clench them into fists. And relax. See how your legs stride forwards: left and right, left and right, such purpose.

Let out a meaningful sigh.

Move aside to let a young couple pass. Observe how

tightly they hold one another. They will be together for a long, long time. Or not. Experiment with a smile.

Hang a left.

Remember your old place at the end of this road; that awful top-floor flat with dark, matted carpet and an extractor fan so loud you avoided going into the kitchen. Recall how you would sit at your desk, concocting plans to build a zip wire that went from your bedroom window into the hospital ward opposite. Another word for zip wire is death slide. Laugh. That was almost three years ago. The bedroom window in your new flat overlooks a bus stop.

Keep going straight ahead, past the barber's, the newsagent, and the frozen food shop. The song in your headphones changes from one of your favourites to another of your favourites. Look up. See how the aerials cluster together on rooftops. Think of the enormity of information being sucked in by each and every one. And think how much you will miss things like aerials when you are gone.

What should you have for dinner?

Pass a guy on the phone outside the pawnbrokers. Wonder who he is and what makes him tick. Keep moving. Check the time on the clock above the library. It is the same as always, stuck for eternity at quarter to six. Enjoy this: it is a wonderful thing. The real time is twenty past five.

Turn right onto a street full of rush hour traffic. Reach into your pocket and turn up the music another notch. Nod your head as the guitars come in. Feel your heart swell with joy.

Pass Tesco.

A little girl is crying outside the Post Office. A man in a duffel coat pulls a silly face at her. Experience a sharp pang of grief and wish you could speak to your father. Tilt your head up to the sky and feel raindrops on your lips.

Remember the night you took half a bottle of sleeping pills. They were herbal and didn't make you tired at all. In fact, they were coated in sucrose and gave you a sugar rush that kept you awake for hours. Watch your step as you almost trip over a ladder in front of the hardware shop. Your favourite bit of your favourite song comes on. Glance into the window at a tin of varnish. Feel a sudden rush of tenderness for tins of varnish.

Step in that puddle just for the hell of it.

You live at the end of this road. Consider winding down some of the smaller streets to your right and seeing where they take you. But worry that if you do that this feeling might go. Picture yourself lying on your living room floor, still in your coat with your headphones on, staring up at the ceiling. Keep walking. Bolognese for dinner. Look at that dog.

As you wait at the traffic lights, try to guess how many seconds it will be until the green man appears. Get it wrong. Twice. Cross the road.

Reach into your bag for your keys. Before you open the door, stop.

Look back at the way you've come. Take in everything from the aerials right down to the pavements. Briefly wonder why the people with the umbrellas look the most unhappy. Then look up at the sky just as your favourite song fades out. Listen to the space in between songs. Think about how much you don't want to die.

Now breathe.

Breathe like breaths are unlimited. Like you will never run out.

You Are Beautiful

The week I decided to express my anger, a capillary burst in my eye.

> We're just getting in touch because we saw
> some crystals and they reminded us of you.

I'd never experienced a burst capillary before. It was painful at first, then it was satisfying, and eventually it was perfect, watching the red bloom across my eyeball.

> We're just getting in touch because we're
> going to mash up some cashew nuts and
> make them into ice-cream and thought
> you might like a snack.

We danced together twice, during the quietest parts of our creative movement class, our bodies pressed together, slippy with sweat, hands searching and breaths like the sea. After the second dance, we went to a vegetarian café. Helmut had the soup, because it was the only thing on the menu that wasn't spiritually toxic. I had a bottle of water, because I was scared my choices would reveal my personality.

We're just getting in touch to let you
know you are loved and beautiful.

Helmut had climbed a mountain that morning. He took his angels with him, he told me, then sat on a rock and got to know them.

'You believe in angels?'

'If you fake it, you make it,' he said with a wink. He ate his soup with his eyes closed.

In bed, we took off our clothes straight away. Helmut had tanned skin and dark nipples. His three long necklaces hung over me as we kissed, and he licked my body like an animal cleaning a wound. My fairy lights twinkled above him.

'I'm scared,' he said, pulling away from me. 'I'm scared to make love to you.'

I looked into his eyes, saw his inner child, and said, 'That's okay. You are beautiful.'

★

Flowing is just getting started. The nerves and awkwardness of being here, sober, in this church hall with these forty people. Dreading interaction, scared you'll do it wrong.

Anybody, any shape, and any age can take part in a Five

Rhythms class. No movement is forbidden, no way that the body wants to move should be denied. Listen to the music as it journeys into your heart. Let the rhythms move inside you.

Your legs are too fat.

Your arms are too long.

Your shoulders are knotted.

Let the thoughts swirl and they may fall away.

Allow your body to grow roots, to twist and turn into the earth. Follow your feet. Experiment with tempo. Feel the feminine energy course through you. Relax your knees. Relax your face. You are liquid.

'No,' Helmut whispered. 'I'm scared for you.'

'What do you mean?'

'I'm scared that if I make love to you, you'll grow attached to me.'

The waves crashed inside me. The heat rose from my gut to my cheeks. Here I was again.

Today on the shrine we have meadow flowers and teacups. Today on the shrine we have a painting of a buffalo. Today on the shrine we have tofu and brown rice.

*

'Maybe *you'll* grow attached to *me*,' I giggled. The giggle that had become one of my defining features, yet felt so little like me.

235

'I'm in love with someone else,' Helmut told the ceiling. 'You are beautiful. Tell me what you want. What is it you want right now?'

'Sparkles,' I said, and he put on a condom.

We're just getting in touch to give you
this emotional cleansing CD.

As he moved inside me, I looked at the photograph of space above my bed and daydreamed. Before either of us climaxed, he stopped. 'What's your darkest secret?' he asked, pulling out.

I have great difficulty keeping my heart quiet and my mouth shut, so I put my lips to his ear: 'I was gang-raped when I was eighteen.'

That photograph of space was taken the year I was born. I was barely a part of that universe, and yet now, here I was. Here I was again.

We're just getting in touch to tell you
this has been a challenging week.

'I can tell you've been abused,' he said, holding a strand of my hair, 'I can always sense that in a woman when I make love to her. I feel like it brings up a certain *abuser energy* in me. Like I could very easily rape you right now if I wanted to.'

I stored his words somewhere safe. I wondered whether

it was cool and groovy that I was with a guy called Helmut and he wore three necklaces and he was saying he could very easily rape me right now. Whether this was all part of some shamanistic journey. Whether we were transforming into something. Or out of it. Whether this was part of something much greater than the two of us.

'Obviously I'm a nice guy,' he added. 'So I'm not going to rape you.'

We're just getting in touch to say
that will be five pounds fifty please.

Staccato is hiccups of emotion. Lust. Terror. Bile. It is false starts and minor setbacks. It is the first screw and the accidental addiction to painkillers, to tarot readings from strangers, to faking your angels and chanting things you don't understand. It is sticking rusty drawing pins into the soles of your feet. It is frustration. It is exposure. Jump.

Breathe in through your shoulders and out through your knees.

Where are your hips?

Jerk.

Feel shock when the act is not as expected. Jump. Feel simmering energy, the flames licking your sides as the sensation grows. Jerk. Let the masculine energy shoot out.

I squeezed his shoulder too hard. 'What's your darkest secret?'

He laughed.

Today on the shrine we have Buddha and a tennis ball. Today on the shrine we have pornography and cigar ash. Today on the shrine we have one grey stone.

★

We're just getting in touch to see whether
you've managed to express your anger yet.

Even the gods have weaknesses. Helmut was a human being.

'I am the love-child of a famous painter,' he confessed.

I looked at the air around his head, and painted it with brushstrokes of mustard, like the oily light in Van Gogh's 'Café Terrace at Night'.

'The famous painter, who happens to be the son of a famous psychoanalyst, used to come to my house for tea,' he continued. 'I was ten years old. My mother would buy three different types of cake, but the famous painter never ate a single slice. I used to sit downstairs, sticking my fingers into the cake, while I listened to the famous painter fuck my mother.' It was all very Freudian.

We're just getting in touch to say
wow, your tits look good in that top.

'I think you should go,' I said. 'I feel weird about something but I haven't figured out what it is yet.'

'Thank you for sharing your body with me,' he said. 'I hope you don't grow attached to me. I am in love with someone else. I could very easily abuse you. I am a nice guy. You are beautiful. Goodbye.'

We're just getting in touch to let you
know you need to fart the anger out
and let the golden light urinate down
your spine.

Chaos is art. Chaos is a squeezing, shaking, spasming loss of control. Chaos is when the capillary bursts in your left eye. Chaos is– Chaos is–

Resist the temptation to shut down. Stay in the moment. Harness your wolf energy. Become part of the mess. Break open. Fuck. Howl.

Chaos is scream. Chaos is laugh. Chaos is rip off your top and sweat, sweat, scream. Chaos is surrender. Chaos is life. Chaos is–

Ray was all dolphin energy. A beautiful man and a good friend. He gave me an emotional cleansing CD and we ate sugar-free vegan yoghurt together.

I waited until my housemate was out then I worked my way through the CD, which was created specifically for women, and involved a lot of touching my yoni and expressing myself through my vaginal opening.

I'm not going to lie: I felt daft. Yelping and flinging my arms in the air, wondering why I felt so raw, why the red in my eyes was continuing to spread.

The woman on the CD told me we were going to sing our anger.

Ray told me I was angry with Helmut because he was the voice of all the men who had abused me.

The woman on the CD told me we were going to make a noise with our teeth.

Ray told me it was time to let it all out.

The woman on the CD told me if I needed to scream, I could scream.

Ray told me to let the anger out through my belly so some of the shininess in my head could sink in.

The woman on the CD told me to go crazy, just go fucking crazy.

Today on the shrine we have blood-spattered blueberries. Today on the shrine we have deer skulls and dandelions. Today on the shrine we have hydrogen sulphide and nitric acid, ready to be mixed and go boom.

★

We're just getting in touch to tell you
we had a really sensual dance tonight.
Lots of us had multidimensional
orgasms and you were missed.

Before my next dance, I took Helmut to one side. 'I need you to know that what you said made me angry,' I told him. 'It's not okay to speak like that about abuse. There's nothing in me that's responsible for other people's desire to abuse. That responsibility is all theirs, all yours, and I need you to know it made me angry.' I pointed at my red, gleaming eye.

We're just getting in touch to say
GO YOU.

'I can explain,' said Helmut. 'I can explain what I meant about my abuser energy.'

I shook my head. 'That's something you need to explain to yourself, not to me,' I said, then I walked away, because some things you don't need an explanation for.

The lyrical section works like an aphrodisiac. It is very likely you will fall in love two or three times in a night, particularly during this stage of the dance. Your hands may fall in love with a stranger's hands. Let it happen. Your love for your own body will be deeper afterwards. You do not need to have sex to be lovers.

We're just getting in touch to remind you
that now you've got part-time work that
will be eight pounds fifty please.

Today on the shrine we have incense and autumn leaves. Today on the shrine we have nectar. Today on the shrine we have a portrait of Nelson Mandela, and a wreath made of black and white feathers.

★

My friend Liza is here tonight. I'm letting more women into my life now I've quit drinking. Women are important. Feminine energy is important. As my feminine energy has increased, I've cut my hair short and got more tattoos. Big tattoos. Fearless tattoos. My body, my choice.

> We're just getting in touch to let you
> know your dance has really changed.

As I dance, I know that I'm both strong and vulnerable. I create fresh movements with my wrists and shins, with my fists and elbows. Here I am. Here I am somewhere new. Here I am again.

In stillness you may experience ripples of where you've been earlier. That is not to be fought against. If you want to crouch on the floor and pretend to be a tiger then do it. If you want to stroke the furniture or lie in the foetal position or spin around on the spot swearing then do it.

Let your soul breathe. Explore the space around you. Find

patterns. Notice that your stomachache has gone. Your feet are grounded. The air between your fingers is warm.

We're just getting in touch because we
want to be touched. Sometimes
touching is all we need.

The woman on the CD told me that finally, we would experience longing. Not a longing for others, a longing for alcohol or drugs or money or sex, but a longing for ourselves. You are what you need. She told me to put one hand on my womb and one on my bosom. She told me to sink to my knees, let myself feel the ground beneath me. Let the earth cradle me.

Today on the shrine we have a looped YouTube video of some babies being bathed. Today on the shrine we have nothing.

Liza holds me close. Her warmth radiates into me. Tears stain my cheeks. My left eye is completely red now, but no longer hurts. 'Forgive yourself for everything', she whispers.

We're just getting in touch. That's all.

The woman on the CD told me that the cleansing process

was complete, but that it could be repeated many times. It is an ongoing project, she said. It is the project of your life.

Liza goes to dance in another space, and I lie down. There, on the floor of the church hall, sweating and shivering, I ask my body for forgiveness. I ask it to forgive me for taking it for granted, for telling it that it is not amazing when it is.

I tell it that it is beautiful.

This Could Happen To Us

'What's this, Mummy?' You point your finger at me. A tiny, dark hair sits on the tip.

'That's an eyelash, darling.'

'Ni-lash.'

'Blow it away and make a wish.'

'*Whhhhsht.*'

'Don't forget to make a wish!'

The moment you were born, I knew you were the most perfect thing I had ever seen. I'd watch you and watch you for hours on end.

I stared at your eyes, as they learnt at first to focus, then to recognise my contours, complexion, wrinkles. Sometimes I'd find that we were blinking perfectly in time with one another, but whenever I became aware of it I instantly lost the rhythm, and my eyes would be open when yours were closed. I'd see the thin, pink veins on your eyelids, and I'd think: I made you. I can't make a cake, but I made you.

'Hello, bluebird,' your daddy would say when he came home from work. He'd take off his coat, and kiss the tops of our heads, and he'd lie on the carpet beside us – his two girls – and then it would be all three of us, looking into each other's eyes.

Sometimes, your daddy would begin to rub my back, or to run his fingers up and down my thigh, and he'd wriggle a little closer, and I'd feel that he was growing hard just for me, and we'd put you in your cot and make love on the bed, there in front of your eyes, except we weren't looking at you any more.

'What's this, Mummy?' Something sharp glints in your hand.

'That's a knife, darling. Put that down.'

'Knife.'

'Put it down, please. Carefully.'

Everyone told us to watch out for the Terrible Twos: our family and friends and the childrearing manuals. *Now that your child is old enough to walk, s/he will need plenty of supervision. Beware.*

We were a little overanxious to begin with, taping over sockets and putting a gate across the stairs, making sure you were within an arm's reach at all times. But as the weeks wore on, we became braver and the trust between us grew. You played in the living room while we were in the kitchen, and we left the gate on the stairs ajar without thinking twice.

My favourite thing about you turning two was that you started to talk to us. Not just sounds any more, but proper conversations. Your personality was surfacing, and your daddy and I loved to work out which bits of you were coming from whom. You were developing my cheekiness, for instance – my wicked laugh and playful verve. And, no doubt about it, you had your daddy's quiet determination. You would never quit at your building blocks, your colouring-in, or your jigsaw puzzle, until you had got everything *just so*, exactly how you wanted. At times, you had your daddy's withdrawn side too. I'd turn around while I was in the middle of writing, and I'd catch you gazing into the middle-distance, with a look that – if you weren't only two years old – I'd describe as melancholy.

'Mummy, what are they?' You're pointing at daddy's arm.

'Um, those are scars, darling.'

'What's a car?'

'A *scar*. It's a place where daddy got hurt.'

'Ouch.'

'Don't worry, they don't hurt any more.'

You looked more and more like us each day.

It was so strange to get used to at first. I carried you for nine months inside my skin, yet you were only half me, and the other half was your daddy.

What an incredible feat he and I had accomplished! Mixing our bodies together like that. Like plasticine: one red block and one yellow, rubbed and kneaded until they were hot and malleable, then rolled together to become the brightest orange.

You're your own person now, and yet you're half of each of us. My eyes. My teeth. My toes. His chin. His cheeks. His hands.

'Darling, what is it?'

You're sitting on the toilet. Six years old now, but your little feet still don't touch the floor.

'Didn't mean it,' you sob.

'Didn't mean what? What have you done?' Your arm is bleeding. Without even knowing I had the first-aid training in me, I raise your arm high into the air and hold your wrist tight to stop the blood flow. I wipe you clean then put on some Savlon and a large plaster.

'Mummy, I didn't mean it,' you say again.

I notice the broken glass sitting on the ledge next to the toilet roll. 'What were you doing?' There's more anger in my voice than I meant there to be.

'I wanted to be like Daddy.'

When you were eight, you asked Daddy and I how we met.

We were taking the bus home from the airport, after a two day holiday to Disneyland (two days is all we could afford), and your question surprised us because we thought you were sleeping.

Daddy was stroking my hair as I leant against the window, but when your question popped out, we both sat up straight to tell the story, as if we had been waiting all our lives for this moment to finally come.

'Your mummy was working for a publishing company,' your daddy said.

'The company that published your daddy's first two novels,' I added.

'Your mummy was a writer too.'

'Your daddy was working on his third book.'

'Your mummy had a rebellious splash of freckles around her eyes. Did I tell you that already? I fell in love with her because of those freckles.'

We continued the story, about how we gave each other feedback on our writing, and how we made each other laugh. And we told you about how one day we talked and talked for so long that we ended up going to get food at an Italian restaurant afterwards, and that Mummy wasn't going to leave a tip but Daddy did, and Mummy knew Daddy must be a nice person because of that.

We didn't tell you the bit about how Daddy came back to Mummy's flat that night, and we kissed for the first time in Mummy's bed, and Daddy lay on top of Mummy as we kissed, and she felt him pushing against her pants, and she knew that Daddy would be a good in bed because of the way he felt against her.

But we did tell you the bit about how Daddy had been a bit depressed ('Why?' 'He was poorly.') and that Mummy had been a bit sad too ('Why?' 'Because Mummy's daddy died.').

You listened to it all, sitting on the edge of the seat, in your brand new Minnie Mouse top, and when we got to the end, you said: 'Was Daddy poorly because he hurt his arms?'

I looked at your daddy and he looked at me, and we both said, in some sort of strange, mangled way that scared us both: 'Well, yes, in a way.'

'Mum?' You're sitting on my bed while I get ready.

Though you've never discussed it with me, I know that now you're twelve you've learnt my make-up ritual off-by-heart. It won't be long before you're copying it for yourself. I feel guilty that you've inherited my eyesight and teeth, and that you're already in glasses and a brace, but I think you're astonishingly beautiful all the same, and know you're going to break hearts one day; including mine, including your father's.

'Mum, did you ever cut yourself?' you ask suddenly.

I put down my blusher brush, with only one cheek done, and look at your reflection in the mirror. You're picking at a scab on your knee.

'Yes, I did,' I say quietly. I've never believed in lying to you; it happened to me too many times growing up, and I don't want you to go through what I did. You'll read the stories I've written about my adolescence one day, though I'll leave it to you to work out which bits are true. 'I didn't do it as much as your father, and the cuts were never as deep, but I did do it. Why, sweetheart? Are you ok?'

'I'm just worried,' you say.

'What about?'

'You and Dad used to cuddle each other all the time. I haven't seen you hug him for weeks. I'm scared he'll get depressed again. Are *you* depressed?'

I join you on the bed, my non-brushed cheek burning just as red as its counterpart. 'Your daddy and I are fine,' I tell you. 'We've been distracted lately; we've both got writer's block. But we still cuddle a lot. It must be when you've gone to bed.' I hold you tight in my arms, rocking you gently back and forth, my scared little bundle of flesh. 'I love you so much,' I whisper, again and again.

And to think we thought *we* were unruly teenagers.

You joined three punk rock bands (because punk came round *again*), stayed out until four in the morning every weekend, and prompted me to call the police three times within the space of a year. Twice because I thought you'd gone missing, and once because I caught you stealing a pair of trousers. I'd wanted you to learn a lesson, but when I got through to the police station, I couldn't bring myself to speak and hung up.

You got *so* drunk too. Your father and I found that the hardest, because it had got us both into trouble when we were younger. Your dad walked down the motorway one night in his pyjamas. The things I did still keep me awake some nights, even now.

One day, I was in the study when I heard you come home from school. I knew something wasn't right because you were sighing and trampling more than usual, banging into walls and muttering under your breath.

'You're drunk, young lady,' I said, instantly realising how much like my own mother I sounded.

'So?' you answered back.

'Were you drinking at school?'

'I'm not talking about it.' You stomped up to your room.

I gave you a few minutes then followed.

I found you passed out on your bed, curled up just the way you had done since you were a little girl. I took off your leather boots and pulled the covers over you. As I did so, I noticed a burn mark on your wrist, and, with a sharp breath, lifted back your sleeve. But there was nothing there.

'I've read your story,' you say to me one evening at dinner.

'Which story?'

'The one you wrote when you were in your twenties.'

I know you picture my twenties as I picture my mum's twenties. In sepia: all muted smiles and echoey dialogue, like some sort of distant dream.

'The one about you getting really drunk and then having sex with all those men.'

Your dad puts down his knife and fork and puts his hand over mine. You've already read his first novel, and told him just what you think of that.

I'm considering asking how you can be so sure the story's about *me* at all, but the fact is, every detail in that story is true, so the challenge would be pointless.

'You know, promiscuity can be a form of self-harm,' you say, taking a sip of water. 'But what they did to you... You're an idiot for not going to the police.'

My eyes fill with tears, and inside I am burning with pain and pride.

On your eighteenth birthday we threw you a big party, with all your friends and family. We spoilt you rotten all day. You were absolutely stunning, in a dress of the brightest orange, and you shocked us by how much of a young woman you looked.

I even got over my fear of baking and made you a cake. Your dad and I made it together. We got flour all over our hands and faces, and kissed between ingredients, your dad getting white marks on my new black dress where he grabbed at me.

After a round of 'Happy Birthday', I brought out the cake. 'Blow out the candles and make a wish.'

'*Whhhhsht.*'

'Don't forget to make a wish!'

I realised then that I would never know what you wished for. My whole life would go by, and I would never know.

When everyone left the party, and it was just the three of us again, we did a group hug. Your dad stuck out his arm and took a photo. We checked the picture afterwards, but the camera had only caught our mouths and chins: three sets of smiles.

★

I was on the subway on the way to work this morning, listening to Chet Baker, to a song called 'I've Never Been in Love Before'. In the song, Chet asks his new lover for forgiveness. He's fallen in love so madly, he explains, that he's likely to appear foolish.

As the song played, I began thinking about my own lover. About the way we met, just two months ago. And the children we might have one day. The questions they might ask.

I thought that I might tell my children about days like today. About how I used to ride the subway to work in a haze, thinking about their father and smiling to myself. And my children would picture those days in sepia: all muted smiles and echoey dialogue.

I thought too about the fact that a fortnight ago, while we were walking in the park, my lover told me he didn't want to live in England when we're older, which I am fine with, and that he didn't want a pet dog, which I am happy about, and that he didn't want children. Because they might turn out like him.

And I've been thinking about it ever since he said it. I've been thinking that I want him to know that what he said is okay, and that even though I guess a little part of me is hoping he might change his mind, it's not eating me up right now.

I mean, we never know what's around the corner, do we? We might not be together in a week, or a year, or a decade.

And then again, we might.

But as Chet Baker was singing to me this morning, I suddenly felt it was important to let my lover know this: that we could end up being together for the rest of our lives, and that we could even end up having children together – if he wanted – and that *this could happen to us.*

And if it were to happen, I think the scars would only make us stronger.

Acknowledgements

A huge and heartfelt thank you to my family: my sister, for her trust and kindness; my mum, for her bravery and generosity; and my dad, who was – and always will be, no matter what – my hero. Thank you also to my grandparents and extended family for their support.

For their feedback and friendship, I would also like to thank: Doug Johnstone, Ewan Morrison, Mark Buckland, Andrew Drennan, Helen Fitzgerald, MJ Hyland, Johanna Green, Ruth Hawthorn, Cherry Styles, Zoe Lambert, Rodge Glass, Cliff James, Daniel Carpenter, David Viney, Ian Carrington, Willy Maley, Janice Galloway, Olivia Chell, Trevor Byrne, Rebecca Horn, Abigail Daly, Nicola West, Katie Anderson, Julian Corrie, Peet Earnshaw, Jenna Omeltschenko, Guy Potter, Ben Wallace, Jo Marsh, Sarah Rowland, Carol Weston, Jamie McIntyre, Chris Grimshaw, Rachel McAdams, Charles Rowley. Thank you to Dr. Chen, Pat on the Manchester Community Alcohol Team, the staff at the Brian Hore Unit, and Anna at Gaskell House. Thank you to the folks at Freight and Blackwell's bookshop in Manchester. Thank you to Socrates Adams. Thank you to my editor Helen Sedgwick and publisher Adrian Searle. Good guys one and all.

The development of this work was supported using public

funding by the National Lottery through Arts Council England. Thank you to the Arts Council, and thanks to the magazines and anthologies that have supported me over the years. A big thank you to my PhD supervisors, Andrew Radford and Robert Maslen, for believing in me – the PhD may not have worked out as planned, but I still learnt plenty along the way.

Thank you to the dancers, the huggers, the holders, the smilers, the swearers, the kickers, the breathers, the lovers, the chanters, the artists, the addicts, the haters, the teetotallers, the belly-laughers, and everyone who's honest and real.

Finally, thank you to anyone out there who has sat with me for coffee, ginger beer, or a good old sob over the past few years. Let's do it again sometime.

Other Acknowledgements

'What Happens When Someone Dies Twice' first appeared in *Litro Online* (litro.co.uk), June 2013.

'Crave' first appeared in *Gutter 07*, August 2012. Permission is granted for quotations from 'Crave': © Sarah Kane, 1998, 'Crave', Methuen Drama, an imprint of Bloomsbury Publishing Plc.

'Daddy Smokes' first appeared in *Causeway/Cabhsair Magazine* Vol. 3 Issue 2, December 2012.

'When I Die, This Is How I Want It To Be' first appeared in *The Scotsman*, April 2014.

'These Little Rituals' first appeared in *Citizens for Decent Literature Online Issue 2* (nowplaying. citizensfordecentliterature.com), September 2012.

'Doctors' first appeared in *Edinburgh Review 134*, June 2012, and reappeared in *The Best British Short Stories 2013*, published by Salt in April 2013.

'Butterflies' first appeared in *Up The Staircase Quarterly* (upthestaircase.org), August 2012.

'A Rough Guide to Grief' first appeared in *Gutter 08*, March 2013.

'If You Drank Coffee' won first prize in the Unbound Press Short Story Award 2012, and was published in the *The Last Word*, an Unbound Press and Spilling Ink anthology, December 2012.

'Let's Buy a Keyring So We Can Remember this Forever' first appeared in *Gutter 04*, March 2011.

In 'Borderline', the diagnostic criteria are reprinted with permission from the *Diagnostic and Statistical Manual of Mental Disorders*, Fourth Edition, copyright © 2000. American Psychiatric Association. All Rights Reserved. Extracts from *I Hate You, Don't Leave Me: Understanding Borderline Personality*, revised And updated edition, 1991, by Jerold J. Kreisman and Hal Straus, are reprinted with permission from Penguin Group (USA).

'For Anyone Who Wants to be Friends With Me' first appeared in *Gutter 05*, August 2011.

'Google Maps Saved My Life' was highly commended for the Dying Matters Award 2012, and appeared in *Final Chapters: Writing About the End of Life* in 2012. It was subsequently published in *Final Chapters: Writings About the End of Life* (ed. R. Kirkpatrick) by Jessica Kingsley Publishers in January 2014. Reproduced with permission of Jessica Kingsley Publishers.

'Like You' first appeared on the Blank Media Collective website (blankmediacollective.org), April 2013.

'You Are Beautiful' will be included in the anthology 'In The Empty Places', due in 2014. This book will raise money for safe houses and scholarships for the victims of child prostitution in Indonesia via the charity Bantuan Coffee Foundation (www.bantuancoffee.org).

'This Could Happen To Us' was shortlisted for the Bridport Prize in 2012.